CONRAD RICHTER *has also written*

Novels {
THE SEA OF GRASS
TACEY CROMWELL
THE FREE MAN
THE TREES — *which is continued in*
THE FIELDS
}

and a volume of short stories
EARLY AMERICANA

These are Borzoi Books, published by
ALFRED A. KNOPF

Always Young and Fair

Always Young

and Fair

CONRAD RICHTER

NEW YORK, 1947

ALFRED A KNOPF

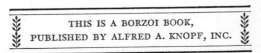

THIS IS A BORZOI BOOK,
PUBLISHED BY ALFRED A. KNOPF, INC.

FIRST EDITION

FOR

Augusta

Always Young and Fair

Chapter One

NEITHER love nor the lack of it kept Lucy Markle from marriage. It was quite another matter, something you might not have entirely suspected or understood at the first meeting with that deceivingly delicate creature of the end of the last century. We have no such pure gossamer handiwork of our Creator today. She was only eighteen but already three of us worshipped her, although I did not count, being only a small distant cousin who cursed his fate that he could never grow up to marry her. I thought when she played tennis that her feet scarcely touched the ground, and I can still see her white dress floating over the uneven, root-bulged sidewalks of Pine Mills light as the vapor in Stephen Foster's song.

It wasn't her lightness but the gentle unbreakable quality of it that made it terrible to reckon with. Knowing her since childhood, I must have felt that soft steel before, but it did not leave a deep enough scratch until the year of 'ninety-eight when I carried the telegram from Will Grail that his cousin, Tom Grail, had been killed in battle in the Philippines. At the depot they said that Frank Dietz, the telegraph operator, called out, "Tom Grail's shot!" while it was still coming in over the wire. It caused a great deal of excitement. Tom was a fair-haired boy of twenty from one of the leading families of the town and extremely well liked. He hadn't belonged to the National Guard before the war but had volunteered when some of the members of our company refused to sign up for overseas. The chief thing about the news which moved townspeople, I think, was that he was the first of our Company G to be lost in the Philippine Islands, which were then as foreign, remote and outlandish as Chinese dragons.

I had been playing ball across the tracks when Frank Dietz called me over and said I better take this telegram to my Cousin Lucy. On the way I told everybody that Tom Grail had given his life for his country, and that the message had come across the Pacific. I passed the large stone house on the terrace where the old Grails lived, and the smaller yellow house of Tom's father, and felt glad I didn't have to take the telegram in there where it would hurt.

I didn't mind taking it to Lucy. She was only engaged to Tom, or so we thought at the time, although later there were some who, in view of what happened, declared that they must have been secretly wed. Others denied it, but most people agreed it was Will that she really loved and that she merely felt sorry for Tom. She had always keenly pitied him. She thought it unfair that of the two cousins, Tom should have been born into a smaller house, a poorer family, to a mother who had never lived long enough for him to know her and a father who was away from home building bridges most of the year. Two weeks before the company left, my mother heard Dick Stengel, the Markle hostler, talking to Lucy out in the yard. He told her that once the two boys were off in the army, Tom would lead a life of hardship, hardtack and hell, while Will would live in officers' quarters like a king. The next few days Will, being captain, was busy on company business; Tom, only a private, was at the Markle house afternoon and evening. By the time Will could find time to come around and explain his neglect, Tom had won Lucy's hand.

Anyhow, that's what folks said. All I definitely know is that when Company G marched from the old wooden armory to the depot, Lucy was there, for I saw her, in a flowered Paris dress, giving Tom presents to take away with him; a picture of herself in a big, white summery hat, a box of green Philadelphia hard-water soap, and a leather-bound Testament and Psalms. The crowd made a respectful little circle about her. When the train was about to pull out, she had let Tom put his blue-clad arms around her and kiss her in front of everybody at the steps of the crowded day coach he would board, while Captain Will had stood looking gloomy and helpless by the steps of the Pullman in which he and two or three of his fellow officers would roll in luxury as far as Mt. Gretna.

Now Tom was dead, and how would Lucy take it, I wondered.

It was an extraordinarily clear and beneficent summer day, the kind Cousin Ruby, who had been abroad a dozen times, called Tyrolean weather. The sky was cloudless, and a bowl of crystal air had come down over the town from the mountains. The great ash trees, lindens and horse chestnuts along Swatara Street joined overhead from one end of town to the other, and under the green arch at the moment a long timber wagon was lumbering leisurely along with rock oaks from the Blue Mountain trailing in the dust behind. A woman from the Big Dam was selling buckets of sky-blue huckleberries from her white-covered spring wagon. And in the big courtyard of the Eagle Hotel I could see a team of farmers' horses standing with dripping noses over the cool, leaking water trough. It seemed impossible to me that on such a peaceful day in Pine Mills a town man could shed his life's blood on a lonely tropical isle half way around the globe and that he would never come back to walk the streets of his native Pine Mills again.

I climbed the Methodist Church hill where the Markle house stood in the very center of town. Since that day I have seen replicas of it in Northern towns and cities as far west as the Mississippi. But in those years there was only one such in the world to me, Cousin Asa's house, a palatial brick pile of three full stories, with mansard roofs and a front balcony with a white balustrade. The house stood back of an iron fence, on

7

a great lawn and with a tall pine tree on either side of the front walk. I let myself in at the pointed gate, crossed the wide veranda and after a moment's hesitation pulled at the large round brass bell handle.

Mary Potts, one of the maids, answered the door.

"Why, Johnny!" she reproved when she saw me. She meant, what did I mean running her to the door when my mother and Asa Markle were first cousins and I could come in whenever I wanted to.

"I've got to see Miss Lucy, Mary!" I said, trying to be important.

Hearing the talk in the hall, Cousin Asa came to the door of his library that lay on the north side of the house. It held among other things a walnut secretary and a great somber bookcase running above it to the high ceiling. You needed a stepladder to get anything out of it, but those large dignified tomes were seldom read. Cousin Asa was a stocky, impressive man with erect bearing, and this together with his noble manner and a trimmed dark brown beard always made me associate him with the future King of England and other monarchs.

8

"That looks like a telegram, Johnny," he said, eyeing suspiciously the yellow envelope in my hand.

"It's for Lucy, Cousin Asa," I said.

In a moment Lucy, called by Mary, appeared on the stair landing, which was wide enough for two chairs and a table. By day a strong prism of light fell on it from the stained-glass windows in the small secondary hall above the balustrade, and now as Lucy passed through it, her dress changed with the colors of the rainbow like the princess in the fairy story. She ran down the rest of the wide, carpeted stairs. As a rule her dress almost completely hid her means of locomotion, and it was a revelation to see her firm legs under that light, floating skirt.

"I got a cablegram for you, Lucy," I told her. "It just came in."

Her eyes, which were very gray, quickly sought me.

"It's from the Philippines!" she said, taking and holding it unopened for a moment in both her hands while the French scent of lilacs she always used came around me.

I saw that her skin, very transparent, was extraordinarily white, with blue veins showing through. Many stronger than she under the stress of a crisis or distraction of sudden meeting with another forget you entirely for the moment, but she glanced at me even more kindly before drawing out the yellow sheet. I hadn't realized before what a fragile and mortal target she was for a missile like this. Then as she read it the delicate blue veins almost disappeared, and I felt that it hadn't been the one for whom she most feared.

For a moment she stood there with the yellow paper between her hands, thoughtful and grave, then she handed it to her father, who had stayed in the library doorway in a kind of fierce and majestic dignity as if to protect her from the unknown. His eyes devoured the telegram at a glance, then flashed at me.

"You took another like this to Jim Grail, I presume?"

"No, sir," I told him. "This was the only one that came in."

His face darkened and he handed me the yellow sheet imperiously.

"Take it back to the depot. Tell Frank Dietz it's a mistake. Tell him I said he should write out a new message and address it to Tom's father.

You can deliver it there." He took a half dollar from his pocket and handed it to me.

"No, Papa," Lucy said gently, and lifted the telegram from my fingers.

"I am only correcting Will's judgment, Lucetta," Cousin Asa declared. "He should have had sense to send it to the boy's father in the first place."

"But it was sent to me, Papa," she said.

Asa raised his slightly bloodshot eyes at me as if resenting my being a witness.

"Take it and do as I say!" he commanded.

In those days a girl from a family like the Markles might demur to her father and try to dissuade him, but almost never did she outright oppose him. Lucy's voice was still gentle, but I could feel the soft steel in it.

"You will do nothing of the kind, Johnny," she requested me.

Under his beard, Asa Markle's face looked warm and red. I knew that when he got enraged, nobody could stand up to him. He was stocky and broad and could break a man's back, they said. Even the tough Irish foreman at his colliery in the Broad Mountain quailed at his temper.

11

But now I saw that the same will that flourished in him was rooted also in his daughter, and that what boiled and burned in his veins was in her delicate and mild, deceivingly so, for of the two today the more fragile was the stronger.

Already she seemed faintly distant from him. She turned to the cross hall where she probably knew that one of the maids stood listening.

"Mary," she murmured, "will you run up and get my black gloves? My best long ones. Johnny, please stay here. I want you to go with me." Moving a few steps, I could see her presently in the large closet under the stairs where I knew she secreted a tiny pasteboard box marked with scrollwork and the word "Paris." Now I saw her take it from one of the old bureau drawers and then peer intently in the mirror as she mysteriously kept brushing her face. When she came out, you could see that her cheeks had faint color.

She pinned on her wide, black sailor, and gently worked on the gloves that Mary had brought her.

"Now, John," she said with pity in her voice, "we must go and see what we can do for poor Mr. Grail."

Chapter Two

A CHANGE in Lucy set in from that day. She looked more sensitive, but more beautiful, too, as if something inside of her had flowered that she had given her heart and hand to Tom while he was still alive. I wish I could transfer to you the feeling that comes up in me now as I see her in an old yellow snapshot, standing on the clay court across from the brick Markle stable, in a white shirtwaist and skirt, her tennis racquet in her hand. Oh, never let anyone tell you that clothes make the person! Lucy's shirtwaist on this day was some crude style of the times. Her skirt was long, heavy and clumsy-looking, and yet the creature within these garments, the inexpressible lightness of her youth and the effortless turn of her hand come up in me and pass through my being like the essence of purest quicksilver.

That picture was taken just before the telegram announcing Tom's death. Afterward she was still lovelier, but she said she didn't care to play tennis any more or ride her side-saddle with her hat up so lightly and her great skirt sweeping to her mare's belly. She still went to the piano, but she played dreamy things or hymns. Even when she walked the street, there was a hushed, delicate quality about her like my mother when she entered church.

Unable to lay a flower on Tom's grave half way around the world, she started taking them to his dead mother's grave in the Lutheran cemetery and to his father crippled by rheumatism and living alone save for his old Pennsylvania Dutch housekeeper, whose only sympathy over Tom was, "Yes, well, that's the way it goes in this world. We all have to die some time." Every other Thursday, when the houskeeeper had the afternoon and evening off with her sister in the country, Lucy took Tom's father his supper. I can still see her walking down the brick, Pine Mills sidewalk in one of her coolest, freshest frocks, with the dainty basket on her arm. Just to see her open that basket would start the saliva in my mouth. First she would lift back the brown wicker lids, then the snowy napkin that was spread over all, and finally the dishes prepared by

Regina's expert hand in the Markle kitchen;
perhaps Regina's own beef broth that had sim-
mered on the stove all day and was now in an old
champagne bottle from which it would be
poured into a fragile cup; half a broiled chicken
or slices of breast; Saratoga or baked potato; hot
biscuits in their own special napkin; a glass of
fresh fruit preserves or wine jelly; and some rich
Markle dessert such as a soufflé or charlotte russe,
all served in Cousin Ruby's gold-band Haviland
china.

With the basket or without, there was something about Lucy now that delicately carried her
affliction without her saying a word. You looked
up and saw her so ethereally patient and with her
you saw Tom Grail. There on your mind's sward
he lay, bloody and light-haired, with an American flag folded over him. Farther back in your
mind you could see him, first standing at the rail
of the transport in the San Francisco harbor,
catching small rolled-up flags and flowers tossed
up to him by women on the Pacific Mail wharf,
and throwing back gold buttons from his uniform in exchange. Next you could see him when
he reached the Philippines, marching in the intense tropic heat in his heavy, blue, Northern

winter coat and tan pants, the wet soles of his army shoes peeling off like paper. And finally you saw him just skin and bone from the hardtack and spoiled cornbeef rations, having to buy back over the commissary counter the packages sent him by friends and hear him tell the others when they bitterly complained, "No use writing home about it. Civilians don't know a soldier's troubles and don't care when you tell them."

And all the while you saw and heard him in your mind, you knew he was dead, like the pictures of men in newspapers, and you remembered the one thing Paddy Emory wrote that Tom couldn't stand was hearing On the Banks of the Wabash.

Oh, the moonlight's fair tonight along the
    Wabash,
From the fields there comes the breath of new
    mown hay,
Thro' the sycamores the candle lights are gleam-
    ing,
On the banks of the Wabash, far away.*

Whenever the men sang it or even played it on their mandolins and banjos, Paddy wrote, Tom would sit with his face on his knees and you couldn't get a word out of him. Underneath he had been terribly homesick, Lucy thought. He had written her once, "I was to Europe last year with Uncle Burt and to Asia this year with Uncle Sam, and all you can give me of the world is Pine Mills."

I can see the whole inevitable pattern of it now, but then my mother thought that Lucy was getting through it wonderfully brave. She went with her mother and father to New York for a week to buy new clothes. Cousin Asa thought her very foolish for refusing to go to any shows, but Cousin Ruby said, "Wait till Will comes home, Ase. Then everything will be all right."

When that day came, I was at the depot. Townspeople kept gathering all morning. It was the usual Reading Railroad structure, painted yellow with brown trim. Soon Frank Dietz gave out the word that the special train was approaching town. All the whistles from Bromley's cider mill to the tannery started to blow, and the church bells from the Old Lutheran to the United Brethren to ring. Small neighborhood groups waited at the crossings, waving and shouting at the heads of Company G men sticking from the windows as the Pine Mills engineer pulled the train slowly by.

At the depot all was excitement. The town band played, while townspeople searched for a glimpse of son or brother, crying out at all the unfamiliar hairy faces that had been smoothly shaven when they went away. I hardly knew Captain Will Grail in his black beard. Only when he opened his mouth and showed his teeth did he look anywhere as young as he really was. He put his faded blue arms around his mother and sister while his father and others waited to shake his hand.

But I noticed that all the time his dark eyes searched the crowd.

"Isn't Lucy here?" he wondered.

"Yes, where is Lucy?" Polly Grail said, looking over her shoulder as if she didn't know.

Around them I was aware of people leaning forward to listen. "He's asking about Miss Lucy," they whispered, and looked around to where the two o'clock Lebanon train always lay in wait, as if Lucy Markle would be found there.

Downtown the people knew better. I saw Mrs. Crider and Mrs. Pumphry secretly watching the Markle house from across the street as Company G approached in a tramping column of bearded men carrying their rifles in such perfect precision and contrast to the tattered and dusty blue of their uniforms. They were on their way to the armory on Mifflin Street. I had cut down the railroad, up over the schoolhouse bank, down the alley and through the gate beside Cousin Asa's fine brick stable, and when Will Grail marched by, striding along at the head of his men in that leaning-back swagger that soldiers don't seem to know any more, the broad white stripes on his blue trousers straightening at every step, I was sure I saw him cast a keen look out of the corner of his eyes at the windows of the front Markle bedrooms. But if Lucy was up there weeping for a fair-haired boy who didn't come back, none on the street glimpsed her. Cousin Asa and Cousin Ruby stood on the triangle of the large front porch, a little formally as if out of loyalty to Lucy, and a little pathetically, too, I thought, while Regina and Mary, with their aprons thrown off, waved at the procession from where the kitchen walk rounded the side of the big house.

Through the armory windows you could see that tables had been set up on long sawhorses, and flags and bunting hung everywhere from the walls and ceiling. The prettiest girls in town waited on the tables, but Will Grail left early. He shook hands with a number of people outside, telling them he was dirty as a dog and couldn't wait till he got home and in the tub.

But his real reason, I suspected, was something else, and I tagged after, going in at Cousin Asa's and sitting at one of the long French windows in the parlor with a book I didn't read. After a while I saw Will coming across the wide lawn between the two houses. In his black beard and gray civilian suit he looked almost foreign. Cousin Ruby must have expected him, too, for she let him in, greeting him warmly while Cousin Asa came out in the hall to shake hands.

"Glad to see you back, Will," he said. "Come in the library and have a drink."

"I will, thanks, Mr. Markle. Is Lucy home?"

"She should be around somewhere. Mary!" he called. "Will you look for Lucetta?"

"I'll get her, Ase," Cousin Ruby said quietly, picking up her skirts to run up the front stairs.

The two men went into the library. I couldn't see them but could hear them laugh and talk. They were in there a long time. Cousin Ruby did not come down again. After a while I heard her call from over the balustrade in the upper side hall.

"Lucy's coming, Will!"

He came out in the hall at once. There were in the parlor two extraordinary and immensely tall mirrors in elaborate gilt frames. They hung above the twin marble mantels on either side of the hall door and ran all the way to the lofty ceiling. In one of them from where I sat I could see part of the hall stairs. They were entirely empty. After a while I heard Captain Will say, "Lucy!" and when I looked up, there she was on the stairs. She was coming down slowly, very slowly, in a simple white shirtwaist and dark skirt against which her arms were almost white.

More than once I had seen them in this very hall with the rugs pulled back, the downstairs filled with young folks from Lebanon and Pottsville, someone at the piano, and Lucy and Will dancing from parlor to library in each other's arms. But Lucy did not let him come that close to her now. She held him at her slender arm's length as she shook hands.

"It's fine to be back and see you again, Lucy!" he said. "You look wonderful."

Her serious face warned him that the old intimacy was gone between them.

"I hope you feel grateful to God for being spared, Will," she told him gravely. "He must have given you a guardian angel."

"I'm sure He did, Lucy," he said, looking at her.

"I don't know who it could be," she answered quickly. "I only wish I could have been more of one to Tom."

His face sobered a bit, I thought, at the sound of his cousin's name.

"I thought we'd see you at the depot."

"Oh, I couldn't. I wasn't equal to it."

"You look very well."

"Well enough. But when I realized you were all going to be here — all but Tom — and march down the street, I just couldn't bear to come."

"You probably looked out and saw us go by."

"No, Will, I was in my room. But I had to

come down now. I want you to come in and sit down and tell me about Tom."

He flinched again at the name, I thought.

"Don't let's go into all that now, Lucy," he said quietly. "It's too far away. Some other time. You don't want — "

"But I do, Will!" she interrupted, her gray eyes begging him. "I must know. Letters don't begin to tell. You were there. You saw him every day. You're his cousin and it's your duty to tell me. I must know everything."

He sobered and when he came into the parlor he had such a grim soldierly bearing and gave me such a stern glance that I would have taken my book and retreated among the palms and ferns but Lucy quickly halted me. It was too hot in the conservatory, she said. She seemed to want me there between them for some purpose. Usually she and Will sat together on the sofa, but today she took a chair. It was a Savonarola chair from Italy, with a V shape above, a V shape upside down below, all delicately inlaid with white. Lucy sat in it like some strange lady with her arms on the chair arms.

Captain Will took the sofa. No matter how she held him off, he was lean and strong and

could take it. He told her very simply how Tom
had volunteered to take a dispatch through
enemy lines and how on the ridge a bullet had
got him. It did not kill and he gave the message
to the friendly Filipino who accompanied him.
Then Tom sat there mortally wounded, shouting
encouragement to the native until he reached his
objective. But when they came for Tom, he was
dead.

They talked for a long time. She asked him
every conceivable question about Tom, hurrying
on to another when the answer hurt. When Will
told her how Tom was buried, describing at her
insistence the lonely jungle scene, and how when
they came back very little trace of his grave remained, she buried her face in her hands. Time
and again he tried to turn the subject to something more cheerful, but she held on to it as if
Tom was her portion and she must torture herself with it.

In the end he stood up with a soldier's decision.

"Now that's enough," he said. "Your father
says you haven't been out horseback for quite a
while. I want you to get in your riding clothes
and we'll go around the Two-and-a-half."

24

"I can't, Will," she beseeched him.

"You must," he said sternly. "I won't take no for an answer."

"Will, I couldn't!" she begged, a shade less imploringly. She looked so slender, pliant and frail it seemed that she was no match at all for his strength, but I thought I could feel those faint steel threads starting to rise in her.

"Nonsense!" he declared. "You need a change. You want to get out of the house. It's such grand weather. You can't conceive how lucky you are living in the temperate zone."

"I know, Will," Lucy said, oh so gently. "But I can't go."

He grew distinctly grave.

"I haven't ridden around the Two-and-a-half myself for a long time," he reminded her. "Won't you do it for me?"

I didn't see how she could refuse him, a returned soldier, but she rose, delicate and untouched.

"I wish it were the old days so I could, Will," she said. "I would have loved it then. But I can't go now. You must understand how I feel."

He stood looking at her silently for quite a

time. He knew and I knew he was beaten.

"I understand, Lucy," he said.

But after he took his leave, I glimpsed his face as he passed the front window, and it held an expression of uncomprehending dismay.

Chapter Three

So far as I know, very little of consequence was ever kept strictly secret in Pine Mills, not even in the brick confines of the big Markle house. Cousins, callers and maids all dripped like leaky taps to the thirsty town. In those days Pine Mills followed its own dramas passionately, the actors appearing in person on its stage. Today we are addicted to the same stories as then, but we take them at second and third hand through the radio and moving picture, and the actors are seldom seen except in bloodless images, much less passed in flesh and blood and bade good morning to on the street.

Everyone in Pine Mills, I am sure, must have known Lucy Markle's story and followed it intensely as a serial. The reader did not have to wait a week or month to know the next installment. It was always imminent, might possibly come today, and meantime additions, missing passages and revealing phases were constantly being filled in by friends and passers-by. There was not one editor or commentator, but many. Most of the town, I think, approved and respected Lucy for her stand, even Will Grail's friends. Death and dignity were taken rather seriously then, and a girl of character stood fast. Lucy was showing her Markle and Grandmother Mattson blood, they said. It would wear off in time, and meanwhile a year or two out of respect to Tom Grail would not hurt her. It was also respect to Company G, to the town which *was* Company G and to the U.S.A. After all, Tom Grail hadn't given just a year or two but the rest of his young and lighthearted life.

I thought that Will took it like an old campaigner. If he grew impatient with Lucy, he didn't show it. I can see his long legs coolly crossing the lawn between the two houses and then spread under a table for a game of three-handed whist with Cousin Asa and Cousin Ruby in the library, but I never saw Lucy make a fourth, although she was an extremely quick and intuitive card-player. Indeed, Lucy was seldom in sight or hearing. I recall one time she came downstairs to pass through the hall and Will sprang up so enthusiastically that he knocked table and cards to the floor. He went to her and for a minute they faced each other in the hall, he dark and hardy, she so blond and gossamery, each reacting on the other, Will's face eager, and hers watchful that she did not remain close to him too long and so impair or perhaps endanger the barricade she had erected between them.

Cousin Ruby sat there pleased. She couldn't help feeling the magnetic currents passing between them. Winter would soon be over. Some spring day the spark would jump the gap, and then they would live happily ever after. But Tom's photographs when they came must have shaken her out of that notion.

I was going into Cousin Asa's one day with a book when Frank Dietz brought Lucy an express package. The Markle house really had two libraries, one downstairs which they called the library but was in fact Cousin Asa's den and sitting room. Here relatives and close friends were taken when they called, the others being formally received in the parlor. The library was a big room with red leather chairs and a red leather couch where Cousin Asa slept every Sunday afternoon. Beautifully bound volumes mostly in sets stood in glass-covered bookcases. The other and lesser library, called the bookroom, was up on the third floor, with open stacks around the four walls. Here were the several thousand books that didn't look too impressive downstairs, the current novels and the older ones of Mrs. Southworth and F. Marion Crawford, Richard Harding Davis, Mark Twain and the many translations from the German by Mrs. Wister, along with the Pepper Books, the Elsie Dinsmore and many others. My favorites were the Frank Nelson series by Harry Castlemon which I had already read several times. They had been bought for Cousin George, who had died.

Today I was up here putting back one G. A. Henty and sampling another when I heard the carriage returning from the Forge. Cousin Asa and Will Grail were in the front seat and Cousin Ruby and Will's mother in back. When I came downstairs, Mrs. Grail had gone on to her own house and the rest were coming in the front door.

"You're just in time to see the pictures!" Lucy's voice called eagerly from the library. "Gutekunst is marvelous. See what he's done with my snapshots!"

They came forward brightening. This was more like the old Lucy, alive and buoyant. She showed them enthusiastically what she had in the package. There was a large picture of Tom Grail in a dark flannel shirt, tan pants, leggings and campaign hat, holding his rifle in one hand and his pup tent looped like a life preserver in the other. The other photographs turned out to be of Tom also, Tom standing as sentry in front of an officer's tent, Tom on the dock, Tom sitting on a camp stool, Tom lying on the grass. There were a number of him as a civilian, too, in the yard, rowing on the old canal, in football suit at Yale and as a small boy skating. But the one we were to remember best was a really excellent enlargement of a boyish and hatless Tom on board ship with the Pacific sun shining on his blond head.

No one said anything much at first, but you could feel the slight chill that had descended on all. After a little, Will murmured courteously that he remembered where this or that scene was taken. Presently he excused himself and left. When he had gone, I thought Cousin Asa would surely say something. He looked very dark and explosive, but Cousin Ruby dragged him off.

The next time I came, photographs of Tom were all over the house. The one with his rifle and pup tent hung on the wall beside Uncle Bob in his Civil War uniform and sword, and the Company G group stood on a high bookcase. As I went up the stairs, Tom's face peered out at me from a little walnut frame on the table on the landing, and when I passed Lucy's room I could glimpse the rest of them on her highboy and stuck all around the mirror of her marble-top bureau. For a week I didn't see the boyish, bare-headed portrait, then I found it in a gilt Florentine frame on the maroon velvet cover of the piano with a low vase of fresh flowers before it. Every day or two Lucy changed the flowers. Will couldn't help seeing it when he came in the parlor. His beard was shaved off now, and I thought he looked a little harassed after his long legs had carefully crossed the path encased in late winter ice or snow between the two houses.

Tom's father died in the spring and at once Lucy took a new duty upon herself. Two or three times a week now you could see her, by early afternoon in the spring, and in the summer toward evening, coming out of the Markle front gate with a basket of flowers from her mother's garden in her hand. She would walk lightly down Swatara Street and then take the yellow clay road up the silent hill. My mother said that after a while it drove Cousin Asa nearly mad. When I passed him in the house and his eyes looked out at me from his beard like some tormented King Lear, I knew she was up there walking among the graves, reading the names chiseled on the stones or sitting delicately on a bird-whitened bench under some gloomy tree, watching and thinking on the peace and quiet of the city of the dead. Of course, he knew that a half hundred other townspeople knew she was up there, too, and were watching and commenting on every move she made, and yet he dare not go up and fetch her in front of everyone. Cousin Ruby looked unwell all summer and my mother thought it was worry over Lucy. From the number of times she was closeted with my mother both at her house and at ours, I knew that something was brewing and soon due to boil.

It came on an August evening. Uncle Albert and Aunt Jessie arrived on the eight o'clock train, and my father sent me for my mother.

"She's up at Cousin Ruby's," he said.

I hurried down the street. It was a warm night.

33

Even a marble statue might have known it by the number of townspeople out on their porches. The whole street was a succession of old and young on rockers, swings and steps. Krimmel's soda parlor was crowded, I could see as I went by, and the red ice-cream flag was out at Mrs. Roeder's, but the only refreshment I had was the cool sound of spring water running into the trough in the courtyard of the Eagle Hotel.

It seemed strange to find no one out on the great triangle of the Markle porch. Inside, the faintly red hanging lamp in the hall was burning, and so was the brass hanging lamp in the library, the one you pulled down to the height you wanted to read by. But no one was there. I went over to the huge parlor. The onyx lamp with the cut-glass shade on the gilt and onyx stand was turned up very bright but no one was there either. The entire downstairs seemed like a lighted tomb. Coming back to the hall I thought I heard voices overhead and ran up the thickly carpeted stairs. They were coming from the upstairs sitting room, the door of which was a few inches ajar.

I was about to burst in when I heard Lucy's

voice. Never had I heard it so quietly bitter before.

"Oh, I know what you mean. I've seen your faces the past year. And you aren't the only ones. Mrs. Higgins came right out and told me I shouldn't go to the cemetery. It's no place for a young girl, she said."

"There are some things we must forget, Lucy," my mother explained. She and Lucy had inherited their gentle dignity from the same sources. It had always made a bond between them. Never had I heard her turn on my mother before. But she did now.

"That's what Papa and Mamma say! I must forget. The war is over and past. That's true enough. No one hardly remembers it any more. Everyone has forgotten Tom and what he did and how he gave his life for his country. But he's still lying over there in the jungle and I haven't forgotten."

"You can remember him and still lead a normal healthy life, Lucy," my mother said soberly.

" But I don't want to lead a normal, healthy life!" Lucy cried. "I would feel like a traitor.

35

I would feel faithless after giving him my promise. I have everything and he has nothing. Can't I go up to the cemetery a few times and live my own life?"

"You pity him, don't you, Lucy?"

Her voice broke and softened toward my mother.

"Oh, I do, Cousin Matty! He never had anything. No mother when he was little. And no father most of the time. He never knew what a home was with that Katarina. He didn't even finish at the university but gave it up to enlist. You know he volunteered just because those few wouldn't take the oath to go overseas. He was only a private, and now he's dead in a heathen grave, and the other boys act as if nothing's happened."

"Everybody appreciates what he's done."

"So they say," Lucy answered. "But no one will do anything about it except talk. And when I do what little I can in his memory, they try to stop me."

"But do you think he would want you to do this for him?" my mother asked quietly.

"Yes, yes!" Lucy cried. "If he knew it gave me peace and satisfaction, I'm sure he would.

I'm sure he does know and appreciates it. Sitting up in the cemetery sometimes I can feel him."

"But don't you think your duty is to the living, too?"

That touched a more vital spot than I suspected. My mother said it with strength and kindness but with shrewdness, too, and I thought I knew now why Cousin Ruby had summoned her to help them tonight. Through the door crack I could see Lucy, standing by the drawn shade.

"Just who do you mean?" She had flung up her head.

"Yourself first, my dear," my mother said. "Then your mother and father. And last but not least, Will Grail."

"I am bound by no promise to him."

"No, but I think you loved him," my mother said quietly.

I couldn't understand the quick fear in her face.

"That can't be true!" she cried as if defending herself from some slur. "And if I had," she went on, "how could I accept him as my husband while I was promised to Tom?"

"But Tom is dead," my mother said cruelly.

"You are just like the others, Cousin Matty!"
Lucy cried. "They all say, now you mustn't do
this! Don't take it so hard! You have your own
life to live. You must go on like you did before.
'First to thine own self be true.' But what they
are really saying is — why do you make such a
fuss over a dead person? He can't go out with
you. He can't marry you or support you or do
anything for you. Forget him. He's no earthly
use to you any more."

"Now we've had enough of this!" Cousin Asa
broke in. I had been wondering how Cousin
Ruby kept him quiet if he was there. "This thing
has been going on too long. Dr. Sypher and I
have a few things to say."

So Dr. Sypher had come, too, I told myself.
They had really banded together against Lucy
tonight. Yes, I could hear his voice now, the old-
time doctor who had brought her and most of
us into our mothers' big walnut beds. Almost before he finished some sage and kindly warning,
Cousin Asa would break in, while Cousin Ruby
and my mother held the flanks. Lucy was quite
surrounded, with no chance to break away. As it
went on and on I marveled how such a slight
fragile thing could stand them off. They didn't

38

mince words. They reproached her for the folly of withdrawing from life, for becoming a pale shell of herself, for holding to a morbid world she must flee before it was too late. More than once she bent like a willow switch under their blows, but always sprang erect again.

Only when my mother returned to the point she had begun when Cousin Asa had unwisely interrupted her did Lucy show weakness.

"And how about Will, Lucy?" my mother asked with her gentle dignity. "Don't you ever feel pity for him, too?"

The others saw the advantage and rallied to the attack. I could feel Lucy wince. As it went on, I felt as when I had to watch a classmate flogged in school.

"Is there no one interested in that poor dead boy any more?" she cried at the end and fell to weeping.

That was the breakdown. In a moment they were all sorry for her and she for them, and Lucy was agreeing pitifully that she would give up the cemetery and be kind to Will Grail again. Little did they suspect, I am sure, what she meant by kindness then. Nor did I. When it came to that stage, I thought Lucy's battle lost and my

39

mother's won. Creeping down the stairs, I called up to my mother to come, that Uncle Albert and Aunt Jessie were waiting for a long time. Then I ran home.

At the lamp post by the Methodist Church I passed Will Grail coming from his grandfather's house.

"Johnny, you're out pretty late," he said, but scarcely glanced at me as he went thoughtfully by.

Chapter Four

WHETHER Lucy regretted her promise to see Will and be nice to him when he called, I do not know, but everyone agreed that she kept it scrupulously enough; that is, under her own rules. I remember the first time that Will called afterward. Lucy and I were up in the third-floor bookroom looking for a novel about the veldt that had apparently been lost. It was supposed to have had something daring and off-color in it, and I think that Cousin Ruby had hidden it. We had gone over half the shelves when Mary came up and said that Mr. Will was down and would like to see Miss Lucy.

I can still see the startled look that flew into her eyes. She told me that if her father and mother were out when I came downstairs, I had not dare to leave. When I gave up looking for the book and went to the library, Lucy hadn't come down as yet. Presently I heard her. She must have dragged every movement of brushing her hair, bathing her face, putting on other shoes and a freshly ironed frock. When she came in the library, Will stood up. He said he thought it would be nice to walk up the Long Stretch, but she countered with the suggestion that they play cards in the library, and that's what they were doing when I left.

It wasn't long until I heard my mother say that she thought Lucy bore an unreasonable feeling against being left alone with Will. If Cousin Asa and Cousin Ruby were out of the house, Lucy would say, "Let's go over to your mother and Polly." If Will wanted to walk uptown, she would stop in for Ruth Higgins or Eleanor Harper, and persuade one of them to walk along. It was an art, my mother said, the way Lucy kept a third person handy at the hour that Will was most likely to appear.

I had wondered at Lucy's quiet cultivation of me until I found that she had agreed to go on horseback rides with Will and that I was being groomed to ride between them. Lucy's old pony, Banty, was to be my mount. He was a sorrel with hair that had tried to turn gray but had only got a dirty burnished look. He was very fat and my legs spread far apart when I rode him. When he grew tired, Banty had a trick of going lame, giving a little dip and jerk with every step. He hoped to be turned back to the stable, but before we left, Cousin Asa told me not to mind the little beggar but push him on. Cousin Asa knew that if I turned back, Lucy probably would, too.

If there was a town in Pennsylvania with more inviting roads leading out of it than Pine Mills, I am unacquainted with it. Westward you could go up the Long Stretch from the middle of town or on the Outwood Road from North Pine Mills. Northward you had the choice of two roads to Cherryville in the gap of the Second Mountain, and eastward you might take the Mountain Road, the Panther Valley Road, the Beaver Valley Road, the Pleasant Valley Road, or the Birds Hill and Auburn Roads. Southward you could choose either the Bethel or the Fredericksburg Road, both of them over the Blue Mountain, or the Swopes Valley or Suedburg Road through Swatara Gap. And you need never come back the way you went, for smaller roads crossed endlessly.

Also, as I remember the roads those days, they were little more than woods and country lanes, charmingly narrow and unimproved. Trees often formed a complete cover, and the roadway kept ever turning so that new sights constantly fell on the eye. If there was a spring in the vicinity, the road veered to it so you could stop and drink. If there was a farm, the road wound intimately close, often passing between farmhouse and barn. We rode through a dappled pattern of shade and sunlight, through fields, woods and water, by settled habitations and lonely stretches, and although I started out reluctantly on that fat old sorrel pony, very soon I considered myself as much a part and parcel of the rides as Lucy or Will.

And so I resented it and resisted mightily when Will took me aside and asked if I didn't want to stay home one day. I told him I had as much right on those trips as he and besides, if I didn't go, Lucy wouldn't either. He only laughed, and I suspected then that something would happen to spoil the day, for it was the Swopes Valley ride, the prettiest of them all.

I wish you could have seen Lucy on her horse that certain afternoon. I have seen her in evening gowns, in tennis outfit and street dress, but never did she appear so much the lady as high on a side-saddle, her body slender and erect, her skirts long and sweeping. There was a gallant quality in the way she sat there, pointed upward, the complete mistress of her mare. Children in the country ran pell-mell across fields to stand like sticks as, waving to them, she rode by.

Our horses went first down past the high yellow bluffs below town, crossed the railroad and old canal, and then across rich bottom land by a noisy stream through a narrow wooded gap in the Swopes Mountain, ever bathed in crisp mountain air. Most of the way Will persistently plagued me. I would have thrown rocks at him if I could have reached the ground. All through the farm lands of the rising valley I had to put up with his badgering. When we reached the summit where the valley is almost as lofty as the adjoining Blue Mountain itself, I raced my pony ahead. I could hear Lucy calling me as I went. Down on the other side, the road led through a very deep hollow with ancient hemlocks on both sides and joining overhead. A decayed rail fence ran on one side and a mountain stream beyond. I pushed Banty through both fence and stream. Fairly hidden there in the woods and gloom, I pulled up, resolved to stay till I was missed and searched for. Indeed, I hoped that Lucy would ride home and spread the alarm that I was lost.

Presently the two riders came by. They seemed unreal, like moving shadows in this dim, forested place. Where the green dusk hung the thickest, I saw Will hold up his hand, and both horses came to a halt.

"Isn't this a beautiful spot?" his voice asked.

I saw him reach out his hand and draw her toward him. She resisted, fighting him for a while, but in the end they were closer than I had ever seen them on the Markle divan. I was amazed how still she lay against his breast. The only movements were the stamping and switching of the two horses, standing so closely side by side. All this time I sat transfixed with rage in my hiding place, my pony cropping leaves and the mountain stream drowning the sound.

After a while I saw Will lift her back in her saddle, and again they moved slowly down the road. What it was I am not sure that I know, and I have been back there since to try and find out, but there was something that day in the dim scene, in the primeval hemlocks standing in their daytime gloom, in the faint sun trickling through the heavy branches of dark green needles like the veriest twilight, and the two figures riding slowly down the deserted woods road that made me feel it wasn't flesh and blood that I had seen at all, but a passage I had read of strange doomed lovers riding through the lone Scottish wood of a Waverley novel.

Still cold with jealousy, I waited for what seemed an hour, but they never came back to look for me, and when I saw them again a mile or two beyond they were riding hand in hand, never expecting to see me behind them.

"Where were you?" Lucy reproached me softly as I caught up to her, giving me a look as if it was I and not Will Grail who had betrayed her.

"Oh, I saw you!" I told them with anger.

"Johnny," Will said gravely as if to absolve Lucy and at the same time ensure her before she might again be lost. "I want to tell you something. Your Cousin Lucy has promised to be my wife."

Chapter Five

So Cousin Asa and Cousin Ruby had their wish, but once they had it, it wasn't quite enough. They wanted a little more. Do you remember the fisherman's wife who lived along the blue sea? When I was a small boy I thought it a dull and foolish fable, but when I grew older I found it a wise and true tale even far from the sea among the Blue Mountains, which the Indians called the Kittatinny or Endless Mountains.

I wish you could have seen Lucy that winter. The secret springs of being flowed up in her again. She was looking on life now rather than death, my mother said. The townspeople felt pleased that the man was Will Grail. Had it been a stranger, they would have complained that he was after her money. I had not realized at the time what an institution Lucy was, in and about Pine Mills, rich, beautiful, traveled, beloved and

48

looked up to as few rich are today. I can still hear
the way townspeople those days spoke the words
"Miss Lucy" and "Miss Lucy's beau." After the
news got out, they smiled to her more warmly
when they passed on the street. A few of the
bolder ones, like Mrs. Higgins or Mrs. Kohler,
who did the Markle washing for thirty years,
spoke to her outright.

I was in the library with Lucy and her mother
when Mrs. Kohler came from the kitchen, wip-
ing her hands on her apron and smiling broadly.

"Well, I hear you're getting married, Miss
Lucy. You're getting a good man. I know you'll
be happy."

"Thank you, Mrs. Kohler," Lucy said.

"She'll be very happy," Cousin Ruby agreed.

But after Mrs. Kohler had gone back to the
kitchen, I saw Lucy look up at the pictures of
Tom on the library wall. They still stared down
from everywhere about the house. She left the
library and from the hall I saw her rearranging
the flowers in front of the photograph on the
piano. After a little I heard her at the keyboard
softly playing and singing a song once much beloved but seldom heard any more.

Only to see you, darling!
Only to hear your voice!
Even the faintest whisper
Would make my heart rejoice.

My mother, when I told her, merely said that Lucy didn't know whether to feel terribly happy for herself or unhappy for Tom. She said that Cousin Asa and Cousin Ruby had wanted a June wedding, but Lucy wouldn't have it because it sounded like a big affair. All Lucy wanted was a quiet little wedding at home. Now they were fighting over whom to invite. Lucy didn't want to invite anybody, Mother said, and Cousin Asa, Cousin Ruby and Will's mother said there were people that Lucy and Will simply couldn't afford to offend. Mrs. Grail had started off with a great hullabaloo about Will's grandfather, who lived right in town.

"If Will wants him badly, he may come," Lucy had said at last very low.

"Then your Aunt Molly. Your mother wants her very badly," Cousin Asa put in.

Lucy inclined her head. As soon as one presented an indispensable guest from his side of the house, someone brought up another from the other side. Lucy sat there still and pallid as china, but my mother said she could feel the first thin fingers of ice such as a cold night throws across standing water.

"Now I will not hear any more!" she cried and ran up to her room.

My mother said that Cousin Ruby told her they had had a long talk after Lucy had gone and came to the conclusion that they dare not bother her.

"She isn't strong and it upsets her when we ask her," Mrs. Grail had said. "She thinks if she says yes to a reasonable wedding it won't be respectful to Tom's memory. I think we should go ahead and do what is decently necessary. If we take the responsibility ourselves, it will save a great deal of friction and agitation all around."

My mother added she understood that Cousin Ruby and Mrs. Grail were sending out the invitations themselves, and most every day one or the other thought of someone they had forgotten.

Lucy's wedding month came round in the wettest May that folks around Pine Mills remembered. Out in the country a vast green growth covered the fields, crowding the fence rows, hiding stone fences, drowning all the small creatures that moved on the land. Lesser grasses choked yards, smoothed paths and matted lanes and road centers, while the greater grasses of rye, barley, wheat and such engulfed farmhouses and barns until they stood deep in an emerald sea. In town it was much the same. Grass marched along gutters, crossed brick sidewalks and rooted in the cracks. It ran to the very edge of buildings, trying to obliterate all that stood in its way. Failing to climb walls, it sent moss up their sides and upon the house roofs. Trees and bushes seemed to bulge with leaves half again their size, brushing the heads of passers-by, hiding houses and closing in windows, until brick, stone and wood seemed conquered, and Pine Mills itself was literally snowed in with green.

In those days out-of-town guests attended events by train, and most of them stayed the night. Indeed, Lucy's wedding was set for six o'clock in the evening chiefly so the trains could bring the farthest guests conveniently to hand in time to change their dress in the provided houses of entertainment. I have heard Pine Mills women cynically observe that a wedding then meant acres of clean sheets, wagons of food, mountains of dishes and silver, and vats of liquor, all of which had to be supplied.

The day of the wedding, Dick Stengel driving the Markle carriage met trains at the depot. So did Grandfather Grail's carriage. I know, for I was sent to the depot to help. The guests that came impressed me. The ladies were in dresses meant to cause a stir in a country town and the men declared themselves pleased to visit again the rural environs of Pine Mills. They seemed jovial over the S. and S. train, which they called the Slower and Slower. The bulk of them were not put up at the Markles' but at the various Grails', at our house, at neighbors' and friends'. On the four o'clock train the caterers arrived from Philadelphia, the darkies walking cheerfully and energetically up Swatara Street while Lib Fidler fetched their great hampers from the baggage car in his wagon.

By late afternoon I am sure that all who lived on Methodist Hill had had their five o'clock suppers and were sitting out on their porches to see the wedding guests go by, the ladies in low-cut evening gowns under capes, wraps and umbrellas, most of the men in tails and high hats. I went around Cousin Asa's house to the side entrance, up the back stairs and down the front to my chair on the landing where I could see everything. An old darky sent by the caterers met everyone at the front door and directed them to the top of the stairs where another woolly darky showed the men to Cousin Asa's bedroom and the ladies to Cousin Ruby's, where they could leave their wraps.

I had not seen Lucy all day. When I had passed her room a few minutes before, her door had been unlatched and I could hear voices in there. Presently Cousin Ruby was called to the telephone down under the front stairs. Almost at once there was a terrific crash from the kitchen, and Mary flew in consternation out of Lucy's room and down the back stairs, leaving the door ajar.

After a little I thought I heard something and looked up. It was my Cousin Lucy. She had come silently out of her bedroom into the hall above me. She looked tall and very pale in the soft, creamy satin wedding dress hung with real lace that had been her Grandmother Markle's. She held the heavy train in her hand. There was no guest in the hall at the moment, and it must have been the darky I had heard mumbling and scraping in deference to such loveliness.

Now she stood at the head of the stairs, her ear bent over the crook in the walnut banister, a look of curious amazement on her face as she listened to the rising surf of voices below.

"What does it mean, Johnny? Who are all these people?" she asked, ignoring the darky.

I noticed she had no slippers on as yet, for the silken-shod toes of one foot had slipped out from under the satin.

"Why, it's your wedding," I stammered.

"But not this crowd, Johnny!" she protested. She stood there a moment longer, her expression faintly chilling the mouth. It seemed to thin her nose and turn the skin milky and transparent as English china. "Will you tell them I'd like to be alone for a little?" she said with deadly quietness and went softly back to her room.

I had no intention of telling that until I had to, and kept to my chair on the landing even after I heard Cousin Ruby return to Lucy's door. She tried it, then knocked sharply. When Lucy didn't open it, the darky stammered what Lucy had said.

"Why, that's preposterous!" Cousin Ruby declared. She called me up to verify it. Her face was still red from hurrying on the stairs. "Lucy!" she called guardedly, knocking again.

"I am resting, Mamma," I could hear Lucy's voice answer clearly.

"But you can't rest now. You must be down in ten minutes."

There was no answer or the slightest sound from the lock.

"Lucy!" Cousin Ruby cried, trying the knob again.

"Yes, Mamma."

"Open the door."

"I can't go down, Mamma."

"What do you mean?" Cousin Ruby's voice trembled a little.

"There are too many. I do not care to face them."

Cousin Ruby turned to me. Her face was white now.

"Get your mother and Cousin Ase," she whispered. "Now go quietly. Don't let on that anything's happened. Cato, will you go down and stay with the waiter at the door? Please do not send any guests up until I tell you."

56

My mother gave me a quick glance when I said that Cousin Ruby wanted her. She probably guessed, for she instantly sobered and left. But Cousin Asa threw me a look out of his beard as he might at a terrier that had disturbed him. Then as I kept doggedly standing by, he closed his lips, annoyed, and moved with dignity for the front stairs. After a respectful interval I followed, taking with me a mental picture of the parlor altar set up in the bay window, of boards beautifully covered with cloth and trimmed with smilax. The Italian lamp burned in the center and four candlesticks had been lighted on either side.

When I reached the upper hall, the door was still fast, judging from the looks of it, for Cousin Asa was pushing my mother away from it. Now he rattled the knob.

"Unlock this door instantly, Lucetta!" he ordered in a tone that would have made his foremen at the mine jump, but nothing happened.

"You must not speak that way to me, Papa," her voice came after a moment gently.

"It will be worse if you persist in this stubborn course!" he said with anger.

"Then I cannot speak to you at all, Papa," she

57

answered, oh, so quietly, but all of us could feel the soft, adamant silence setting in.

Cousin Asa stood there helpless for a little.

"What in God's name has got into you, Lucetta?" he begged her. "You are not sick?"

"No, I am well, Papa. But you and Mamma knew I could never go through with a big wedding."

Cousin Asa gave his wife an accusing look.

"It isn't a big wedding, Lucy!" her mother entreated through the crack as to a child. "There's no best man, no bridesmaids. It's at home as you wished. It's very quiet and simple."

"Then who are all these crowds of people?"

"We told you whom we were inviting, Lucy."

"No, Mamma," loving but deadly, "I should never have given in, had I known."

"You saw all their gifts."

"But I didn't dream they would be coming."

Cousin Ruby shook her head, and Cousin Asa took out his watch.

"Lucy! We can't stand out here like strangers and argue with you through a locked door. You must open the door, or I shall have to break it in."

"Sh, Ase, please!" Cousin Ruby begged him. "Let Cousin Matty talk to her."

For a time my mother reasoned with as much dignity as was possible through a door crack, joined presently by Will in his evening clothes, his tie drawn to a perfect bow. If they could have got Lucy angry or crying, then I felt there would be some hope, but her voice stayed unbreakably gentle and mild. They tried by every means to get her to let them in and talk to her face to face. Lucy said she agreed with them, that she despised people who locked their doors like children, but she couldn't let them in. The other time they had broken her down and had their way. This time she was resolved not to let her convictions be torn and trampled in front of everybody. She asked Will to forgive her. He must remember he had his life and family. Poor Tom had nothing but her. She could see him now looking at her from a dozen pictures, and she would not debase him before all these people.

I still have the feeling that if Will's mother hadn't come up, my mother might have found a way out, for Cousin Ruby was thoroughly frightened now and willing to promise anything, and my mother said afterward she meant to beg Lucy and Will to go out the back way to the Methodist parsonage, where the minister would meet them and quietly tie the knot. They would have needed to come back to the house only for the wedding dinner, or merely to look in on the guests if they wished. She felt sure Will would have assented. But Mrs. Grail, when she came, burned the pudding. She had pale chestnut hair without a gray thread and was a woman of great personal charm. When she sat down and talked to you, she had a way of devoting herself entirely to you, shutting out every other person and subject. It was as if you, when she spoke to you, were the only person in the world worth talking to and she the most understanding. I thought at the time that if anybody could persuade Lucy, she could, but now when she began devoting herself with great affection to Lucy, it suddenly became nothing but a trick. The moment she said, "My daughter!" I thought I could feel the gossamer steel threads rising, multiplying and cross-strengthening on the other side of the door.

Meanwhile six o'clock had come and gone, and a growing silence downstairs revealed the knowledge and consternation that something untoward had happened. When I looked down, I found a group of upturned faces at the foot of the stairs. In the end I skinned down and out of

Cousin Asa's house the back way, going home by Mifflin Street and the dark railroad so no one would see. The doors at home were locked, and I sat on the back porch till the rain put me to sleep. I knew that if I sat in the front, people would stop and ask why I wasn't at the wedding.

It was late when my mother and father and our guests came home. My father woke me and ordered me in. I knew by his grave eye in the light, by my mother's utter weariness and by the guests' strange behavior that this time Lucy and her Markle will had not been broken.

Chapter Six

I SAW Lucy out on the street next day as if nothing had happened. Her step was more floating than ever. There was no hint that she had done any untoward thing.

"Johnny," she greeted me delicately as we passed.

After a few steps I turned and looked after her. So had others on both sides of the street, I noticed. When I went on I saw Will Grail standing on his side porch watching her too, until the Methodist Church descent hid her from sight.

You might have thought that Will Grail would have felt bitterness for Lucy because of what had happened but he told my mother that he blamed himself for everything. He said that if he had had his wits about him, he would have run off with Lucy to Maryland long ago, and let the devil take both their families. My mother thought he still meant to do it at the first opportunity after the affair had quieted down. Meantime in September I was bundled off to prep school in New Mexico for my health. It was too far to come home for the holidays. When I did return, it was a Saturday evening in June, and I didn't see Lucy or Will until at church Sunday morning.

The Methodist Church of Pine Mills was built mostly by Cousin Asa. It is a large colonial brick structure with the most noble steeple in town, a hand-carved design of the four façades of a miniature white church, each with its own slender spire. It had always given me a little shock when miners fresh from the miners' train lifted their black fists at it and poured on it the most terrible of curses. The story ran that while it was building, Cousin Asa had taken a contribution from each of his fourteen hundred men at the mine, deducting it from their pay envelopes. Indeed, old Billy Flowers, when he was drunk, used to stand and point out to passers-by the bricks that belonged to him. But my mother declared warmly that the story had no truth in it, pointing out that there wasn't a miner who didn't treat Cousin Asa with great respect, which was entirely true.

The Markle pew stood third from the front on the left center, that of the George Grails on the right. As a small boy I had often watched young Lucy sitting near the end of her pew with Will managing to be just across the partition, over which they exchanged glances, whispers and notes. Cousin Ruby and Cousin Asa were in their pew this morning, and Will, who must have come ahead of his family, sat in his accustomed place by the partition. But Lucy was notably absent.

Not until we were in our seat did I catch sight of her. The choir box stood in the right forward corner of the church, and in the forefront at the organ facing the pulpit was Lucy. During my year's absence in New Mexico I had wondered at times if my boyish fancy might not have overplayed her. I was fast becoming a man now, and my values in life were changing. But today when I saw her again, sitting there at the organ, I realized that, although I had crossed the continent twice in the meantime, I had seen no one to challenge her, and I pondered what distant strains of blood must have fused in her to make a creature of such extraordinarily fragile and lovely power.

Will Grail did not smile when we shook hands

after church, and that puzzled me a little. But after I had been home awhile, I found that Lucy was fairly throwing herself on another. Morning and evening worship, prayer meeting, Christian Endeavor and Sunday school were her lover now. My mother said that to see that lovely young girl go to church almost every day like a nun, to have her waste her white fingers on the keys of a wheezy church organ and forgo all the harmless pleasures and pastimes of her youth, had made Cousin Ruby actually ill and Cousin Asa blasphemous. Sooner than have had this happen, he told us he would gladly have seen the church he had built consigned to the bottom of his black, flooded thirteen-hundred-foot level.

The second or third winter I was in New Mexico, Cousin Ruby passed away. I knew, of course, that she was never the same after what happened the night of the wedding. But then she had always been a little on the unwell side, puffing on the stairs so that as a child I used to think the chair on the landing had been placed there so she could get her breath on the way up. Ever since I could remember, the Markles had spent three or four weeks at French Lick in March and April, so I gave no thought to it when I saw in the *Herald* that they had gone there more often and stayed longer. The day I had the news, Cousin Ruby was already buried, and although I was two thousand miles away, I could plainly see her grave in the shadow of the great dark family monument, and I felt a little sorry that she would have to lie there among all those grim old Markles whose fierce enlargements I had often seen hung in the library or piled up in the third-floor storeroom.

The following June when I came down Swatara Street, the big house looked as it always had. But when I opened the front door, I imagined faint traces of gloom up the magnificent staircase, and in the depths of the brilliant parlor shadows that I hadn't remembered being there before.

Then Lucy came walking out in the hall to see who it was, her step so quick and light and something about her so untouched that whatever I thought had been lurking there was instantly dispelled. But when I saw Cousin Asa in the library, I had a little shock. His great strength seemed broken by Cousin Ruby's death, and it was plain at once that he leaned heavily on Lucy. He told me he had just been dictating to her. My mother had already told me that she kept the house now, planned the meals, kept his books and wrote his letters for him. I could see such a letter lying on his walnut secretary at the moment, complete with his name, all in Lucy's fine copperplate flow, the crosses of his middle name, Mattson, flying like the lightest of pennants some distance from their masts. Cousin Asa had a horror of forgers and would sign his real signature only on important documents and large checks, never where it might be seen and copied by some unscrupulous person.

Once that vacation and twice the following summer Will came over while I was there, but Cousin Asa didn't welcome him as I had seen him in the past. He was too dependent on Lucy to wish to lose her. Also, he was having trouble with his eyes. I can still hear Lucy's voice reading to him. She read him the daily papers from end to end, the *Philadelphia Public Ledger* and the *North American* in the morning, and the *Evening Bulletin* and *Miners' Journal* at night, he on one red leather chair in the library and she on the other. He also drank a good deal more than he used to, and Regina and Mary were not permitted to serve him. Lucy had to mix it for him.

I used to think it a fascinating picture to watch the gentle and devotional Lucy pouring Scotch whisky from a sinister-shaped bottle into a glass of cracked ice and then siphoning the soda in, often touching the glass to her lips to see if she had the desired flavor.

Some had the cruelty to say that this was the cause of his death, after they found him at the bottom of an old unused shaft at the mine. But Dr. Sypher quickly pointed out that Asa Markle had been half blind for several years, and the men at the colliery confirmed it. Nevertheless it was a terrible thing for Lucy when she first heard it, and a worse thing when they brought him home. It was lucky, everyone said, that Will Grail had just returned from camp at Mt. Gretna. He came over to the Markle house the minute the news reached him. He took complete charge, and at the grave stood close beside Lucy as if to restrain and support her. She looked so slender and stricken, her face through the black veil the whitest I had ever seen it. Will seemed like a solid rock by her side, the very shape and mold of the man she needed, and a good many said it appeared to have taken Cousin Asa's death to bring these two together again.

That's what I thought, too. When we got
back to Lucy's house, I found it was Will who
had charge of the customary funeral luncheon.
He knew how to run an army mess and had got a
vast lot of food together as well as townswomen to
prepare it so Mary and Regina could attend the
service, and now he walked around with his soldier's eye and bearing, seeing that it was properly
served, first to the immediate family in the library, then to the many out-of-town guests in
dining room and parlor, and finally to the country folk on benches which had been set for their
comfort in the side yard. By the time he had
made sure that the last humble stragglers were
fed, the will had been read by Judge Connors in
the library.

I can still see Will's face, and thought it grave
when word spread of the size of the estate left to
Lucy. We all knew that Cousin Asa had been a
rich man, but we had no idea of the list of stocks,
bonds, mortgages, houses and farms he had
owned, not counting his Kalmia mine of famous
red-ash coal with its miles of underground work-
ings. Now before they left for their homes, those
who had done business with him in the past,
bankers, fellow directors, colliery bosses, tenants

and debtors, went in to pay their respects to Miss Lucy. Not all were content to withhold their problems. More than once I saw Will Grail come to the library door and glance with dark inquiring eyes where Lucy sat at Cousin Asa's secretary, silently listening to some matter that concerned the estate. On one occasion I saw her take her pen and run a line through the amount on the books a poor debtor owed her. But she did not glance up or seek Will's help now. In the end, as if he felt the broad, glittering and incontestable stream separating him farther and farther from her, he turned and crossed the lawn to his own house.

Chapter Seven

FROM that time on we were aware that something had happened to Lucy. What it was, we did not know at first. She had given up playing the organ at church after her mother died. Now she gave up attending church, or any other public or private event, and began more and more to lead a solitary life. My father said she could have bought a great town house on Spruce or Pine in Philadelphia and lived like a queen, but she continued to stay on alone, except for the servants, in the old house at Pine Mills. She hardly changed a chair in it. When electricity came to town, she was practical enough to let them put in a plant at the colliery, but in the house she kept on using the carbide system her father had installed before he died.

After the first few years we began to notice that Lucy's dress stayed the same. Always well ahead of Pine Mills styles, she began to appear behind them. My mother urged her to go to New

York or have Miss Sally Werner, the dressmaker, come in, but Lucy said there was nothing
she needed, that she had closets full of clothes.
The only new thing that we knew her to buy was
an oil painting of Tom which she hung in a massive gilt frame on the parlor wall. The red Rambler that Fred Jones of the Jones garage had used
to drive Cousin Asa back and forth to the colliery, she kept standing unused in the stable. She
walked tirelessly instead, as many did in those
days, mostly alone, over Birds Hill, up the Long
Stretch, down to Exmoor or through Squire's
Woods, a familiar figure in pleated shirtwaist
and oyster-colored linen in summer, and in winter wearing her brown-streaked sable cape, stopping to speak a few words to every child, or to
give a kind pat to a horse or dog. She was especially partial to young girls around the age that
her Sunday-school class had been, and on occasion
she would ask them along on a walk, which made
them feel signally honored and pleased.

There was something in her walk that was un-
forgettable. When young girls were along, she
always kept a little ahead. She seemed almost in
flight from them, as if they and Fate might be
forces that would drive her toward Will if given

a chance, and that her only escape to Tom lay in the past. With her ancient skirts almost to the ground and in her favorite straw hat with bird plume, even the humblest country folk who saw her pass knew her and her story.

My sister told me that once when they stopped before a farm gate near the top of Pleasant Hill to look at the view, the farmer and his wife came out and begged Lucy to come in and rest herself. The woman fetched milk from the spring house, and all the time they were there the farmer and his wife looked at her with pity in their eyes. The farmer's dog came and put his jaw on her knee. There was no doubt that people and animals alike were drawn to Lucy, and it struck me that the same inexplicable power which formerly made her seem to float in the air now came out in a different way, as if there continued to be distilled in her some essence of life that beings sought and fed upon.

I remember a school song we had when I was a boy. A bar went something like this:

> Everyone that knew her
> Felt the gentle power
> Of Rosalie, the prairie flower.

The sweetness of the words had always offended me. I thought them trite, cheap, the product of some sentimental mind, and we boys had disliked to sing it. But when I grew older the conviction fastened itself on me that the writer must have really known someone like Lucy.

It would bother my mother to see her moving alone down the street, or going into her empty house, but renouncing the world had its compensations. Summer after summer when I came home from college I would marvel at Lucy's scarcely touched youth and beauty. Of course, her clothes and formal manner gave her an ancient appearance, and her hair had turned a kind of beige gray from the day her father had been found in the shaft, but it had been such a light shade before that at a distance you couldn't tell it had changed. And when she came closer, her but faintly faded cheeks were so smooth and the step of her high lace shoes so effortless that you had the impression her hair must be still blond. Indeed, as the years went by with scarcely little change from one to another, it seemed to me that her particular refuge must hold the secret of youth, and that the inescapable processes of growing old had no power over her.

All this the town noticed as well as I, and never stopped speculating that she and Will would eventually get together. People pointed out that neither Miss Lucy nor Will had ever married. I was too inexperienced then to understand that a town has the benefit of the pooled wisdom of a whole community which in its history has seen about everything, including more than one long-deferred courtship. All I thought of were the times in the past I had seen them in each other's arms and that now the nearest I saw them together was once when I had caught Will pacing like a paid watchman by the lonely Markle house at night. Of course, he must have seen her by day, too, and what the sight of her ancient skirts and her monstrous shirtwaists with their wasp waists and starched, high slanted bosoms did to him, only God knew. I had often wondered why he continued to stay and be tormented in Pine Mills.

I had finished college and was a young mining engineer at the colliery when Lucy asked me down one Sunday afternoon. She was my real boss these days, and I thought it was to talk over some business matter, but I was mistaken.

"I'd like you to walk along with Will and

me this afternoon," she said, coloring slightly. "He's leaving tomorrow and I couldn't refuse him."

"He's going for good?"

"I don't know," Lucy said delicately.

"I thought Cettie said a bunch of kids were going with you today."

"They were, but Will asked me if I could excuse them. He has something he wants to say."

I pricked up my ears.

"Did he say where he's going?"

"To Canada, I think," Lucy told me, her voice very careful. "He feels that he should join up."

So that was it, and I resolved at once that I would never go along and stand between her and Will today, much as I would have liked to see him. For several months, I knew, he had been chafing at the bit, telling everyone that we must get in it. He was still captain of Company G, Pennsylvania National Guard. Now at forty he was giving that up for a foreign cause to serve in what capacity he might. I admired him tremendously and did not see how Lucy could do otherwise.

He dropped in presently, and the young girls

shortly afterward. They were about the age of my baby sister, Cettie, around eleven or twelve, and we had to sit there in the parlor and wait while Lucy told them her plans had changed and they couldn't very well come along today. They were visibly disappointed and she served them ice cream and cake as a consolation. They sat rather awed in the big Markle parlor, on the edge of chairs and sofa, impressed to be served by a uniformed maid. Nearly all, I noticed, had chosen the side of the room from which they could see the portrait of Tom Grail. It had been painted by Mrs. Jenkins, who used to spend her summers in Pine Mills where she might be seen daily about the streets sketching with her class of young people. She had copied it from the photograph that used to stand on the piano. It was a large and striking likeness, and more than one woman of Back Street had bribed Mary or Regina to let her see it when Miss Lucy was out.

It was plain that the girls today wanted to talk about the painting but didn't know how. One of the bolder asked if Miss Lucy didn't think the European war terrible, and that started it. But it wasn't of Will, who was going to it perhaps to die, that Lucy spoke, but of Tom, who had gone to an entirely different and now almost forgotten war. I could see the girls were familiar with the story, and now you could feel their excitement that Miss Lucy was talking to them personally about her dead lover she had remained faithful to all these years. Was that he in the painting, one innocently asked, and then the questions flew, leading Lucy on and on through the whole heroic story, to which the questioners eagerly listened as if they had never heard it before.

It seemed to make her only more ethereal and beautiful to tell it. There was in some of the old stock of the better families of town a certain temper of hospitality that has almost disappeared. My mother had it, and I have often seen her display it, but I don't know how to describe it except to say that when a situation rose to bring it out, especially if the person were hostess in her own house, the most unlikely and unpromising mistress of this quality would become astonishingly more that her usual self, finer, more animated, radiant, almost exultant with love and care for her company. But I had never seen anyone who had it with such brilliance as Lucy this afternoon. She was like a sparkling spray.

All the time Will sat quietly listening. He

seemed to take pleasure just watching Lucy. If it seemed strange to him to have them make such a fuss over Tom's picture while he sat there neglected in the flesh before them, he gave no sign. He was the old soldier. He knew he was also the old rejected lover. Then he had known Lucy a long time and probably knew what to expect. Indeed, I was the one who grew restless at last and retired to the library. When the shadows began to fall and it was too late to go for a walk even if Lucy had released her guests, which she hadn't, I saw Will across the hall get up quietly from his chair to go.

Lucy accompanied him to the door, where they stood only a yard or two from my chair.

"I'm sorry, Will," she said. "But I couldn't send them away."

"It's all right, Lucy," he told her. "I just wanted to ask you something. Are you happy as can be expected? Will you be perfectly all right while I'm away?"

I saw her look at him, but whether with sudden fear or pride I cannot say.

"Why should you say such a thing?" she murmured.

"I simply wanted to make sure before I went,"

he said gravely. "If you'll tell me, I'll feel better in my mind."

"Why, of course, I am perfectly happy and fine," she told him. "And able to take care of myself," she added.

"I'm relieved," he said, and held out his hand. "Good-by, Lucy. God be with you."

I thought, as I went out after him, that she, not he, was the one who should have said it. But then life was seldom what it should have been, and my Cousin Lucy even less so. I remember following Will outside, shaking hands with him by the iron gate and wishing him luck. When I looked back at the house, Lucy had closed the door. I can still see Will there under the tall, somber pine trees, and the purplish red hue of the bricks of the big house beyond. I believed I knew now why he had never left Pine Mills. Had he felt that in her state the last years she might some day need him, and he wanted to be near to help her? If he had, I thought, then love was least of all what it should have been to make two people faithful all these years to such separate and futile causes.

Chapter Eight

I T was when Will came home from Germany that we learned he had finally given Lucy up. He had been away for nearly five years, had gone over to his own country's forces when we entered the war, and was a full colonel now, the first that Pine Mills ever had. But we heard that those four strenuous years in France had taken their toll and brought on a recurrence of the tropical ailment he had picked up in the Philippines nearly twenty years before.

All he wanted from this time on, he said, was peace and quiet. His father had been dead before he left, his mother buried about the time of Château-Thierry. Polly was married and lived at Baltimore. Now he took over the old stone house and settled down to the life of the confirmed bachelor. Those who went in the house said that army routine had left its strong mark upon him. Everything had to be just so. Even the magazines were kept in perfect formation on his library table, one overlapping the other as in a club. He had a housekeeper who came in by the day and slept outside. When she was out, he took his meals over at the Hickory House.

It gave me a little shock when I heard about his first meeting with Lucy. My sister, Cettie, said they met in front of Hal Bradley's store. Will stopped, shook hands, asked politely about her health, then went resolutely up the street, refusing to look around. How would she take this, people asked, and what would she do? It was almost as if he had jilted her. But if in Lucy's breast there were any wounds from Will's defection, she concealed them well. I would look at her sometimes as she went down the street or about her stale round of duties in the old house, and her graceful breasts, once so soft and mysterious-looking, appeared resigned, flat and sterile as a nun's in my eyes. Oh, there wasn't a poor needy horse, dog, man, woman or child in Pine Mills who didn't receive the benefit of her charity. Mary and Regina claimed the town didn't know half the times Miss Lucy dug her hand in her pocket. Every day now since old Mr. Seibert had died she had carried dinner to his widow, who lived alone and helpless in her white house downtown.

But so far as Will was concerned, Lucy asked for no quarter and gave none. Her loyalties lay elsewhere. She had made her bargain and would stick to it like her father. Once when I had been with her, she had stood silently before the painting of Tom on the parlor wall. As she turned away she had said to me:

"All is forgotten today, Johnny, but I don't forget."

And never did she. When money was to be raised in Pine Mills, she could always be counted on for a generous sum to head the list. It was seldom, if ever, in her name. She simply wrote on the paper: "To the memory of Thomas Grail, $100," or whatever the amount was. That's the way it appeared in the *Pine Mills Herald*, and everyone who read it knew who had given the money. She kept speaking his name in quiet reminder to business callers and to women she would graciously stop to speak to on the street or country road. If she came on a group of small boys with their heads wet from swimming, she would pause to tell them, as older ladies did those days, that they must be careful in deep water, and relate the story of how a Pine Mills boy would have drowned if another boy hadn't dived off the bridge and saved him. And when people complained, she would remind them how a Pine Mills soldier in the Philippines had to eat spoiled food, pay for his presents from home, wear shoes that peeled off like paper and then give his life for his country. She had a whole fund of such stories. Often she didn't mention the name, but they all knew it was Tom Grail, that the company was Company G, and the bridge the stone arch of the Little Swatara.

All of us agreed that Lucy's mind was keen as it had ever been. Those of us connected with the business of the estate could go to her with a problem and she would grasp it and dispose of it quickly as her father. But as far as she was concerned, the World War had never happened and the Spanish-American War just closed. Her stories were not of the long dead past, but as if they had taken place only yesterday. There was, in the way she told them, a delicate yet significant relationship between her and her hero. Tom had been just a youth, and so was she, for she was still younger than he, his betrothed and companion. That was where I began to get the idea that perhaps here lay the cause of her never seeming to grow old. The mirror in her room was so covered with snapshots and a band of black velvet ribbon, I am sure she could see little or nothing of herself, only the flower of Tom's youth and of those happier days in which she still lived. If deep in her heart she knew otherwise, she never let such treason rise to her higher mind, putting aside every bit of evidence, always believing against belief.

All that fall she and Will remained to each other as if living at opposite ends of the town. I remember looking in as I passed those two large houses, silent and almost empty, next door to each other. Together with their wide yards they occupied more than half of the long block, and when you started under the row of trees that stood in front of them, you had a feeling of going into the shadows. Once I had seen the sun shining brightly on both houses, but now it was going down. The early yellowing of the horse chestnuts helped. From the middle of summer on, and sometimes even earlier, the mossy brick sidewalk was strewn with withered brown leaves. As fast as they were swept up, others fell. Inside the iron fence, both yards looked perfectly kept, yet verging on decay. Seldom by day could you see life in either of the two houses, and by night the blinds in the few lighted rooms were drawn.

That was when the town, I think, gave up the last hope of Miss Lucy and Will ever getting together. Next spring the new American Legion home was finished and they decided to call it the Tom Grail Post. It caused only local talk but a great deal of excitement when word got out that Miss Lucy planned to attend the dedication. Townspeople refused to believe it. Of course she had given five hundred dollars toward the home, and it was she who had kept Tom Grail's name green all these years. But people pointed out that Miss Lucy simply did not go anywhere. Why, she had not attended any social or public event for nearly fifteen years!

On the day of dedication a March haze hung over the countryside so that the Swopes, Blue and Second Mountains looked a faraway misty blue. Even in Pine Mills you could smell the pleasant odor of farmers burning brush. We had planned to hold the services inside, but the day turned out so mild and sunny that we changed it to out of doors.

As the hour approached, a crowd fairly cov-

ered the terrace yard of the Legion home and
spread to the sidewalks on both sides of the street
below. I think that Miss Lucy had drawn many
of them. They wanted to see for themselves if she
would actually attend. She had not yet come
when Company G in full regimentals paraded
from the armory led by the drum corps and followed by a column of lively blue and yellow caps
of visiting Legionnaires. Prohibition was still
among us, but numerous bottles had circulated
among the men, who were filled with comrade-
ship and the spirit of celebration. They called
off-color French phrases to each other as they
streamed up into the yard, where they broke out
into songs they had learned on the other side.

Will Grail made a mild effort to stop them but
they drowned him out. This was their day, and
they had just swung into a particularly bawdy
and shameless verse of Mademoiselle from Ar-
mentières when a loud "Sh!" rose from the
townspeople. I heard the singers behind me sub-
side, then shut up the visiting Legionnaires.

When I turned around, there was Miss Lucy
mounting the terrace through the crowd as only
a lady can. She had on a long, formal blue afternoon dress over which hung her best cape with

its golden sable collar, and on her head a rather wintry toque with sable to match. I think it was something in her distinguished, ancient clothes, in the way she carried herself, and especially in her unshakable, fragile face that stopped the obscenity. Through the growing silence Chaplain Dalton met her and escorted her across the yard and up on the porch steps to the chair reserved for her by the speakers' table. On the wall above her hung the painting of Tom Grail she had loaned to the post for the occasion.

I could feel the instant effect of her presence on the townspeople. It was plain that the dedication had assumed new importance in their eyes — and drama, too, for here together for the first time in many years were the three figures of that celebrated local triangle — Miss Lucy and Will in the flesh and Tom in oils. Lucy always had that rare thing, presence, and today her face held something spiritual. She had been vindicated, and now she sat there in delicate and holy triumph.

Through the services her upward posture never changed. She held her head as if every word was sacred. The day's speaker was the state commander, a square, energetic, tough-faced realist. He paid the usual enthusiasms to the late war, to liberty and the Legion. At the end he threw his energies to the heroic Pine Mills soldier after whom the post was to be named, recounting almost in Lucy's own words the familiar story of his death in action.

Then he paused and looked up at the painting.

"I had these facts from a well-preserved, gray-haired lady. She's our guest of honor today. You may guess how long ago they happened by looking first at her and then at the young boy she was going to marry. . . ."

When I glanced at Lucy, she had drawn back as if something had struck her. Her eyes stared around like eyes that had never seen this place or people before. I saw that her face was ghastly. She seemed to be mysteriously stricken. When the speaker finished, she took advantage of the polite applause to let herself into a fit of coughing so violent that she bent her head low with the seeming ferocity of the spasm. Holding the handkerchief to her mouth and still coughing, she rose, turning her back on the speaker. She did not look at Will, who was gazing puzzled at her, but moved to Chaplain Dalton, who had risen with her. With the handkerchief still pressed to her mouth, she apparently begged him to excuse her, for he nodded with concern and helped her down among the silent and troubled crowd she had to pass through to get to the street.

I had elbowed up to her, and when she recognized me, her hand clutched my arm.

"Johnny, I am ill!" she said in a strange, low voice behind her handkerchief. "Please take me home."

"I'll get my machine," I told her.

"No, I can walk," she said. "Don't look at me so, and people won't know. Let's go as if nothing has happened."

I did as she told. She was still very white. I could feel her shaking inside. Hardly had we left the post when Cettie came hurrying after. She was in high school now and had been watching from the Shomo window across the street.

"Lucy! What's the matter?" she begged.

"My dear," Lucy murmured gratefully. "Please take my other arm. Now let us go together."

It sobered me no little. Not since Cousin Asa's death, and not even then, had I seen Lucy so dependent on anyone. Silently we aided her to the big brick house and into the dim hall.

"I'll call Mary!" I promised.

"No! Not a word. I think I'm better now."
Lucy halted me, and I knew that if I wouldn't
help, she would go up herself, one hand on the
banister and the other on Cettie's arm.

All my life I had been familiar with Cousin
Asa's stairs, but today, with Lucy ill, it seemed
that I was seeing them for almost the first time.
The table and chair still stood silently on the
wide landing where Lucy paused to rest a moment, something I had never known her to do
in her life. Colored light from the stained windows in the side hall over the balustrade fell
across her white face, giving her the look of one
of the early women saints. Indeed, the stairs
seemed like those of an ancient convent or clois-
ter today, gloomier than I remembered, the air
close, heavy with the redolence of old carpets,
bedding, upholstery and especially of lives once
here and now vanished, while a thousand and one
household objects of the Victorians still remained, continuing silently to age and shed their
odors and faint, ghostly emanations of the past.

These past years Lucy, of course, might have
made any room in the great house her own, but
she had chosen to live like a nun in her old bed-

room. I had not been in it for some time. Now I saw that she still had on the bureau the sterling silver-backed toilet set that Tom had sent her from San Francisco. The bristles of the brush had been beyond use for years, and at places where the hand must hold them the thin metal of the other objects had been worn through. The striped cream and green shades were three-quarters drawn as usual, but I could see that the snapshots of Tom tucked all around her mirror were darkened with age.

Cettie and I meant to help her to her bed, but she pushed us aside and went on to the bureau, where she tore the black velvet band from the mirror and stood there leaning with her hands on the marble top, staring into the glass.

"Johnny," she said, "will you hand me the Florentine frame?"

I knew she meant the picture of Tom from which the portrait had been made. It used to stand downstairs on the piano, but when the painting was hung in the parlor, she had taken it to her bedroom, and here it was now on the highboy. The framed picture had faded a little, but the Pacific sun still shone warm on Tom's light hair and his eyes looked out young as ever over the low blue bowl of hepatica and bloodroot she had before it.

When I gave her the picture, she just took it from my hand and held it up in front of her against the glass. I could see her eyes move searchingly from the incredibly boyish features to her own reflection. Then she turned to me as cruel and tragic a face as I ever expect to see in this world.

"How do I look? Don't deceive me. Tell me precisely!" she commanded, terrifying us a little, for this was no Lucy we knew.

"Why, you look a little pale, Lucy," I told her.

"I don't mean that. How old do I look?"

I glanced at Cettie, whose eyes questioned me, and I knew there was no help from that quarter.

"I can't tell about other people's ages, Lucy," I put her off. "I never think about yours."

She slipped off her cape and handed it to me to lay on the bed. When I turned back, she was pushing up the sleeves of her Alice-blue dress. Her bared arms looked white, incredibly white. She held them forward and stared at them in the glass.

"Are they still young and lovely?" I wasn't

93

sure to whom the words were spoken, but they were in such despair, and Cettie didn't answer, so I had to.

"Yes, of course," I told her.

"Lovely enough to hold their lover?" she demanded.

"Why, yes, I'm sure," I stammered.

"You're lying, Johnny!" she cried at me, and turned to her namesake. "Whatever you do, Cettie, don't be false to me. How old do I seem to you?"

"I don't know, Lucy," Cettie said very low. "I think Mother said you were forty."

"And Tom, how old does he seem to you? I don't mean as he looks on here. This was taken more than twenty years ago. I mean in your mind today."

"I don't know exactly," Cettie whispered. "About my age, eighteen or nineteen."

Lucy looked as if Cettie had slapped her.

"If he came in here alive tonight," she went on as to an enemy, "whom would you expect him to be interested in, you or me?"

"I don't know, Lucy."

"Of course you know!" Lucy told her ruthlessly. I had never seen her like this. "You and your friends have often thought about him. I can see it in your eyes."

"Well, yes, we have thought about him some-times," Cettie admitted. "Because we heard so much about him."

"Tell me!" Lucy cried.

"Well, I guess he would run around with our crowd."

Lucy's eyes blazed. She looked as if she could destroy Cettie, and me, too, for good measure.

"You can go now," she said after a moment. "Thank you for bringing me." But there were no thanks in her voice. "Go on!" she cried as we hesitated to leave her. "I wish to be alone in my house."

As we crept reluctantly down the stairs we heard the key turn in her lock.

"Now don't say anything about this!" I or-dered Cettie and let her go.

For a while I waited in the hall downstairs, hoping to hear Lucy ring for Mary or Regina. Not a sound rose. The great house stood around me like an empty shell. I had the inescapable feeling in here that it was late in the fall with winter not far off. But as I stepped out of the door, I saw through the wilderness of bare gray limbs that a red maple across the street had come out in flower. There used to be in Pine Mills a number of these native trees, one great trunk occupying most of the sidewalk on Mifflin Street, and the effect of their leaves in October sunlight was of a blinding brilliance. They are still more beautiful in the spring, I think. This one directly across the street from Cousin Lucy's had no hint of leaves as yet. Examined closely, the flowers are very slight and unimpressive. In a vase they look scanty indeed. But seen at some distance and especially among other leafless and barren wintry limbs, the whole tree appears to burn with the delicate red flame of awakening life and spring.

Chapter Nine

FOR two weeks Lucy did not come out of her house, and no one saw anybody go in except Miss Sally Werner, the dressmaker.

"She's sick, Miss Cettie," old Mary told my sister when she wanted to run in and ask about Lucy but found the front door locked. Indeed, even now Mary would open it only in inches.

"Why is Miss Sally coming then and not Doc?" Cettie threw back at her, for she resented a maid shutting her out of her own cousin's house.

"Miss Lucy sent for her," Mary said, making ready to close the door. "I'm sorry, Miss Cettie, but I have my orders. She told me not to let anybody in. Not even you or Mr. Johnny."

Cettie wouldn't pass Lucy's house after that. When she came downtown, she crossed the street at Hutton's and went down the other side, crossing back again at Will Grail's corner. But I didn't mind going by when I came that way. I would loiter a little, looking up at the windows, wondering how the old girl was making it and when I could take up with her several matters about the colliery. The two tall pines looked dark as crows, each standing on one long leg. They seemed ancient and a little moth-eaten, as if time was running out on the Markles.

Saturday morning we heard that Dr. Showalter had been called to Lucy's bedside, and when I got home from the colliery Saturday noon, old Charley Fisher was waiting to see me. Charley was the trusty runner of errands and bearer of tidings among the better families of town. Never was he said to betray a secret, and I saw by my mother's face that she had learned nothing of his mission from him as yet.

"Colonel Will wants to see you, Johnny," he informed me gravely.

"It's about Miss Lucy!" my mother declared quickly. "She's worse, Charley?"

"I haven't seen her, Miss Matty," he said with grave respect.

"But you must have heard," my mother insisted.

"Miss Lucy never was stout," Charley admitted. "But she always had a good constitution. I think she'll get through all right."

"Did Will see her?"

"He didn't say." Charley looked at the floor gravely.

"Well, what did Doc say?"

"I think Doc's still out in the country, Miss Matty," Charley said. "He passed when I was going in Witmer's store this morning."

I shook my head at my mother. She would never learn anything from Charley. Indeed, he kept her secrets as well as he kept others' now.

"Tell Will I'll be down," I told him, "soon as I eat my dinner."

Will Grail's house, I reflected as I approached it, was still one of the most beautiful in town. It was also one of the oldest. Aged men asserted that it had been the original Hickory House about 1820 and that the little stone stoop on the side street had once been the entrance to the barroom. This Will's mother always vehemently denied, declaring that her Grandfather Butler had built the house himself and that none but Butler blood had ever lived in it, certainly not a tavern-keeper. Old men would nod gravely and sympathetically when she told them, but privately they

99

went on calling it the Old Hickory House. Smaller than the Markle pile, it was a Georgian house, two and a half stories of yellow fieldstone. Some autumns the great ash trees on the corner and in the yard turned the very golden color of the masonry, giving the walls a most curious effect, as if part of the house had become fluid and free to move in the wind. Unlike most stone houses, it bore a shingle roof.

The front door had side lights together with a fanlight above, so that the hall need not be dark by day. Now I saw Will himself coming to answer my bump at the heavy dented brass knocker.

"Come in, Johnny," he said, and took me into a room with the door to the side street. I had not been here for a number of years and looked about for any sign that it might once have been a barroom. If it had any such markings, they were well concealed today. It was Will's library and sitting room now. An old-fashioned red clock ticked placidly on the mantel. My eyes confirmed that he kept his magazines meticulous as in a club. Even the hassock he had pulled up to his favorite chair seemed perfectly in its place. The *Philadelphia Press* lay in exact folds atop one another on the floor by his chair, and a Scotch and soda stood on a small table by the chair arm. The house seemed calm, with an austere and orderly bachelor peace.

He asked me to sit down, and we talked awhile on baseball and other subjects. Then he lifted up his glass, took a strong sip and set it down again.

"Johnny, your Cousin Lucy is pretty sick. Wouldn't you like to see her?"

"They won't let me in," I told him.

"I think they will," he said thoughtfully. "I understand she's asked to see me, and I thought it would be nice if we went together."

I had to admire the way he said it. His purpose, I thought, was plain, but he hadn't said a word that involved him. There ran through my head all the times that Lucy had been the one to take me along. Then he had been the objector. I thought that times had indeed changed when the shoe would fit the other foot. But all I said was that I would be glad to go with him.

"Good enough!" he nodded. His face did not confirm his satisfaction. Rising, he emptied his glass with the air of a man who felt he would need it. He did not ask if I would have any. Stepping to a mirror he tightened his belt, straightened his tie and patted his hair. He looked like an old, rusted and somewhat jaundiced soldier with an encounter ahead that was not as welcome as it once might have been. Although we were going only next door, he got his hat and at the door turned to me. "Now, I don't think you and I should tell anybody what's said today." Then we went out.

I had been aware, of course, the moment we went into the front hall that he did not intend to take the old, long unused path through the hedge between the two houses. Instead we took what in Pine Mills we called the pavement, the front sidewalk, where everyone could see us. We turned formally in the iron Markle gate and up to the front door.

Old Mary thrust out her head.

"Oh, it's you, Mr. Will," she said, pulling the door wide. "But he'll have to stay out," she added, meaning me.

"He's my guest, Mary," Will told her quietly. "I asked him to come along." He stood back. "You go ahead, Johnny."

Mary's face looked bleak.

"You have to tell her yourself then, Mr. Will. I don't dare to. You better wait till I call you."

We went into the library. The room was very

still, the shades drawn. Not a sound could we hear of Mary's feet or voice upstairs. Even autos and wagons on the street outside went by muffled as if we were underground. Each of us had taken one of the big old leather chairs. And now that light and sounds were shut out of the library, it seemed that other things came in. For the first time the dim grandfather clock above me seemed like something once alive instead of an instrument of wood and iron. There it stood unusually tall, shrouded in shadow and silence, aloof, withdrawn from this world and life as if dead to the present and living only in the past. I had always thought of this room as cheerful and pleasant, but today, with the house closed, it had a strange musty smell, almost of the tomb. The shapes of furnishings and table and mantel ornaments reminded me of dusty objects shut up in some ancient castle, objects extinct to this world and of meaning only to the ghosts and phantoms of another day. Some of those phantoms were looking down on us now with their veiled eyes from frames on the library wall. Most of their names and connections I knew, the stories that had come down of their good deeds and bad, of their quarrels and funny stories that did not seem so funny now, what this one had said to that one when they were living, and what they had left and to whom when they died. Many of their possessions were still in this house shedding their influence over the one who remained, and for the first time it came over me what a wholesome thing it was that God in His wisdom decreed that man and woman must some time die and slough away from all these rotten old birth wrappings, must sever themselves from hoary carpets and massive beds, from antique chairs and antiquated bureaus, from moldering furnishings and endless stuff in cluttered attic and stable, leaving all cleanly behind to disposal and eventual destruction.

Then old Mary came to the door and we went up. Had it not been for the colored window, the stairs would have been still darker than the library. The thickly padded carpets swallowed our steps. It was like the sick house I remembered as a boy just before George, Lucy's brother, had died. I had been taken in to see him and not a sound had dared to be made from parlor to stable. Now I showed Will the turn in the hall and Lucy's door. It stood ajar. He braced himself, knocked briefly and nodded to me to follow him into the sickroom. But I stepped just inside the door and stayed there.

Only the older generation today knows what such a room was like, the dark paper and darker woodwork, the lofty ceiling, the drawn shades and motionless hangings, the dimness and the close hush. You could hardly believe that the world had ever come in here, that gay notes had once been written from the staid mahogany bulk that opened into a venerable desk or that a lively young girl used to dance in front of that ancient marble-top bureau's mirror. The lounge chair with its footstool, the small cushioned rocker, the low chest for bed-clothing and the other chest by the window for shoes all bespoke age and the past. And the soft aura the moment you passed the threshold was that of a maiden lady, the floating emanations of very old silks and out-dated toilet powders, the fragrance of old lavender, of old-fashioned soaps, and of rows of scented clothing that had hung in the closets for a decade or two.

I thought for a moment that Will stood confused. Then he moved courageously over to the spool bed where Lucy lay. All you could see of her body was the slender ripple under the covers and her white face on the pillow. I was astonished at what the mysterious illness had done to her.

Will tried to be brisk and cheerful.

"Here, here, Lucy! This is no time to be sick, in the spring."

She lay for a minute just looking up at him. Her eyes had never seemed so large and dark.

"I've prayed to be well, Will," she said, very low, and I could see at the foot of the bed her Grandmother Wilson's mahogany kneeling stool with its stained crimson velvet pad and rack with an open prayer book.

"You will be," Will promised her. "What does Doc say?"

"He thinks I'm a little better today."

"I'm sure you are," Will said confidently, but it was just a farce, all three of us were aware.

She lay so still watching him. I had known Lucy all my life but never had I seen such purity in her face. It was as if everything else had been burnt out, leaving the soul itself to look through. I had seen that look once before, on a schoolgirl sick with what the doctors then called spinal meningitis. Our class went in a body to see her, and that was the way she had lain and looked at us from her bed.

"Will," Lucy begged. "I'm sorry if I troubled you, but I had to see you."

"That's all right, Lucy. I wasn't doing anything," he said quietly, but a little sternly too, I thought. It seemed to make her more pitiful.

"Please pull up a chair, Will. I want to talk to you. I've been lying here the last few nights thinking. Will, do you remember the song we used to sing in school:

> And the long afternoon
> Together we'll pass
> When the clover is growing,
> Mill May, Mill May."

He didn't say anything and she went on.

"It made me think of that time you and I came down the alley together from school. We were just little, in the intermediate, I think. We went in the stable and Dick wasn't around, so we went up and lay on the hay. We could hear Prince and Roderick chewing down below. Do you remember?"

I couldn't see whether or not Will inclined his head. He had not sat down, and now he stood there with his head bent a little as if in appeasement, but the rest of his body looked adamant. Lucy went on.

"Last night I thought of the time we skated to Exmoor. Do you remember that? It was very cold. We were on the canal and you told me the Swatara was frozen over. We sneaked off from the others across the towpath. I had never seen the creek frozen solid before. It was wonderful skating on and on and never having to turn back, and the way our skates rattled over the riffles. We went between hemlock banks. The creek was always turning ahead. We said this was how it must have looked to the Indians. Then near the foot of Swope's Mountain I broke through, and you picked me out and built a fire on shore between the young pines and hemlocks. It was like a room. Nobody could see us and I took off my skirts and shoes and stockings and put your reefer around my legs and you dried my things and burnt one of my shoes a little, but nobody but us ever knew."

I could see her head move on the pillow.

"Will!" she cried faintly. "What have we two done to each other?"

I don't know whether or not Will ever regretted his plan to bring me along. He stood stiffly composed and controlled for a little. Then he glanced back gravely and appraisingly to where I stood, and that was the first time, I am sure, that Lucy knew I was there. She raised her head, staring at me across the room, and I fancied that the steel I knew so well came into her eyes.

"What are you doing here, Johnny?" she asked sharply.

"He came with me, Lucy," Will told her. "He hadn't seen you for a long time."

"Well, he has seen me now. He can go," she said without pity. Only once before had I heard her like this, the day Cettie and I brought her home from the Legion.

I turned to leave.

"Wait for me, Johnny," Will said. "I'm coming right away."

"He must go, but you needn't," Lucy whispered.

"I'm afraid we've been here too long now," Will declared. "I hope we haven't tired you out. I'm sure you'll be better in a few days."

I waited stiffly outside the door, but I don't think she asked Will again to stay.

"Good-by," she said at length, so low I could

scarcely hear her. "Thank you for coming to see me, Will. I'll ring for Mary. She'll let you out." Far down in the subterranean rear of the house, I thought I heard the bell. And when we reached the landing, Mary was at the foot of the stairs, opening the front door so we could better see to descend.

Chapter Ten

WHEN we left the house I wasn't sure that I expected again to see Lucy alive, but I didn't tell my mother. Of course, I knew she would want to know everything the moment of my return, so I took supper at the Hickory House and didn't go home until a late hour when I knew she would be in bed, and although she called me into the bedroom, it was difficult to cross-examine me then. Mondays and Tuesdays the collieries never worked until orders for approaching winter accumulated and Sunday and Monday I started at every knock. Tuesday when I went downtown I saw old Dick Stengel spading up a Markle flowerbed with a fork, and from that I judged that Lucy wouldn't be dying.

"Ground looks rich, Dick," I said for something to say, opening the iron gate and stepping in.

"Ought to with all I put on it already," Dick grumbled. "But the ground don't work so good. Getting old like everything else around here."

Now what did the old walrus mean by that, I wondered. Suddenly I heard my name called. Looking up I was surprised to see a strange young woman at the edge of the great triangular porch. Have you ever found yourself suddenly reliving an experience of your childhood, as if your small self was alive in you all the while and the only trick was how to step back into time and find it? It was something like that when I saw this person in the bright spring sunshine. For a moment I thought it was Lucy as I had seen her one day long ago when she was a young girl and I a small boy. She had been to the third-floor storeroom that we called the attic, streaked her face with dust to make it look older, and put on one of her mother's discarded gowns, pinning up the skirt, which was much too long, and the effect of such a slender and exquisite child in a masked face and huge fantastic dress gave me a boyish emotion I can still feel.

Now today I saw it was indeed Lucy. Her old-fashioned dress had been shortened by Miss Sally but only to her shoetops, which, we learned afterward, was as far as Lucy would let her go. In its original length the dress had had dignity and a stately sweep, but now abbreviated it showed Lucy's high button shoes and struck me as grotesque. For the first time she looked older, I thought, and weary of life.

"Hello, Lucy," I said. "How are you?"

"I am better," she told me in a voice so unlike that of the Lucy we knew. "Did I hear Cettie? Will you tell her I would love to see her?"

"I'll tell her, Lucy," I promised. "But she isn't here and I don't know if it will do any good."

"Why won't it do any good? I need her. I wish her to do something for me."

"Well, you know Cettie," I said a little uneasily. "I'm afraid she won't be very anxious to do it — under the circumstances."

Lucy's eyes fixed themselves on me. They had a mild, diffused, slightly staring quality I had never seen in them before.

"Then I shall have to go and talk to her myself," she said resigned. "Will you wait for me, please?"

I was aware that old Dick had stopped his spading.

"Wasn't that Miss Lucy?" he asked when she had gone back in the house.

In a few minutes she was out again. She had put on some outlandish hat and thrown over her shoulders a lightweight cape which had not been shortened, for its points almost dragged on the ground. Her step through the iron gate was not too strong. After she had gone up the sidewalk, I saw town women come cautiously out from under the fly of Hartenstine's butcher wagon to speak to each other in low tones as they looked after her.

Ordinarily I would scarcely have believed it, and it seemed very curious indeed when she returned twenty minutes later and Cettie was with her. They hove into sight around the pale green clapboards of the Keefer house, walking quietly, talking mildly together. You would not have suspected that Lucy had ordered her out of her house only a week or two before. But as they came to the gate Cettie gave me a meaningful glance.

"Will you come in, Johnny?" Lucy said thoughtfully. "There are things I want to ask your opinion on."

Today the shades in the library were up, and I

was concious that something had changed, but for the life of me I couldn't tell what it was.

"I have been thinking," Lucy informed me oddly. "I must do something about the old house. I don't think Will likes it as it is. I have been thinking about going to New York, and Cettie shall go along with me."

I should have been surprised, for Lucy had not been to New York for fifteen years, but I wasn't. I could understand now her rapid conquest of Cettie and how Cettie must have argued with my mother to let her off from school. Now Lucy led us slowly in a kind of ritual from room to room asking if we didn't think a new paper or a brighter-colored woodwork would be an improvement. Max Sikes of Pine Mills had always done the Markle painting and papering, but the paper was imported and bought in New York. More than once I had heard Cousin Ruby say with the infallibility of the rich that she would have nothing but English papers on her walls; they were expensive but never did they fade. And now Lucy reminded me of a slight, younger and yet strangely older edition of her mother as she led us from room to room, laying her hand on a wall where the paper had cracked and asking if we didn't agree it would be wise to replace it.

When we came to her room, it was Cettie who noticed it first.

"Why, where are all the pictures of Tom?" she cried.

At once Lucy turned on us. For a moment a semblance of her old steely self lived and I thought I could feel the acids working in her as they had that day several weeks before.

"Don't either of you ever speak that name to me again!" she warned us bitterly.

I thought it a most unusual and inexplicable thing to say. When we came downstairs, I saw now that the other pictures of Tom had vanished, too, and that was what had puzzled me in the library. Of course, I knew that Tom's painting was still at the Legion post, but I had thought it Lucy's neglect or her illness until today. I am not sure that I ever heard her voluntarily mention Tom again. When by chance his name came up and she was present, I could see the fine hard lights blazing far back in her deceptive gray eyes as if he had done her some terrible and irremediable wrong.

But today in a moment it had passed and she

was herself again. She called Mary and had us
served sherry and some of Regina's inimitable
cake in the library. But her talk was not the
bright and spirited chatter we knew. She didn't
mention going to New York again, and when
Cettie asked her about it before we left, she
looked vague and said she would let her know.
That was the last, I think, we heard about her
wanting to go to New York and take Cettie
along. It seemed to have become clouded over in
her mind, and when I asked Max Sikes when he
was going to paint and repaper the house, he said
he knew nothing about it. Lucy hadn't spoken a
word to him.

It troubled me, but not so much as the curious
interest that Lucy had lately begun to take in
men. As a girl she had never been the coquette
but rather the butterfly. Men in general hadn't
meant very much to her. It is true she was pleasant enough to them, but you had the feeling that
her civility was kindness on her part, that she
barely glimpsed them as they passed. This was
especially true since Tom had died. Now, however, when men spoke to her she appeared
pleased and would stop and chat with them on
the street. She seemed to distill a fine pleasure

from contacts with the roughest characters, and asked me once if I didn't think George Hubbley handsome, which startled me a little, for we had just passed him coming from the miners' train, and I didn't see much in him except a hard-drinking young miner with a tin bottle and bucket slung over one shoulder and coal-black face and hands.

Just the same I didn't expect any trouble. Everybody in town knew her and would pity her, I felt, rather than anything else. Besides, she was Lucy Markle. It never occurred to me that someone far below her might misunderstand, particularly some fellow like Tom Widener, who lived down by the bridge. Why, when Cousin Asa was alive Tom Widener wouldn't have dared to come into the Markle kitchen, and now because Lucy in her button shoes smiled and chatted as they chanced to walk up the street together, he came along like a bull through the gate, in the front door big as you please and into the library that the likes of him had never seen before.

Exactly what happened I never asked. Since Cousin Asa's time there had always been a table of bottles standing in the library for the hospitality of guests, and I believe that Lucy gave him a drink or two when he asked for it. But after she found what she had on her hands, she stood up like a Markle and ordered him out of the house, and when he drunkenly refused to go, old Mary ran out the side door for Will, who came over and threw Widener out. It caused a stir downtown, but I didn't hear about it until I arrived at the colliery next morning. Then in the afternoon when I came home from work, Cettie told me that I was invited to Lucy's for dinner, or supper, as she still called it.

It was a dusky evening and Lucy's dining room was lit only by a pair of candles, but even if I hadn't been told, I would have known that something had happened. There was an air of excitement about her that I hadn't seen for a long time. I thought she looked younger and brighter. Her cheeks had color and she held her head at such an alive and artistic angle. The centers of her being seemed to have been mysteriously stimulated, and I wondered how an unpleasant incident like the Widener affair could possibly have been translated in her into such delicate animation. As the meal went on, I felt her grow more restless. Her changes of position became frequent and eager, and when the clocks struck the first quarter after seven, she rose.

"Will you walk along up for the mail, Johnny?" she begged.

"I'll run up and get it for you," I offered.

"No, thanks, I'd like the air," she said quickly.

I would rather not have taken her to such a conspicuous place so soon after the Widener affair, but I understood now that she meant to go and that this had been her purpose in inviting me to supper. She slipped into her cape before I could help her and into the closet under the stairs. Her perfume ever since I could remember had been the faint fragrance of French lilacs, but now evidently she put on some heavier scent, for when she came out the thick odor of musk preceded her. It was so unlike the Lucy I knew that it annoyed me, but the liquid in her eyes swam so tenderly on me that I could say nothing.

The seven-thirty mail was the chief event of the Pine Mills evening. It was the heaviest incoming mail of the day and even before the sacks arrived, townspeople began to congregate. This was where couples met and formed for the evening, and until the windows were opened, the small lobby would be filled. Greetings, talk, news and social pleasantries flew so that it sounded like Sunday school or a big party. Most everybody with a lock box had their doors standing open, and while they talked would reach an arm through the crowd to extract letters as they came. I think this is what gave such a peculiar spice to the affair, everyone packed bodily against everyone else, all watching their own boxes as they chatted, enjoying the excitement and lottery of seeing letters pop here and there while behind the glass the mysteriously blurred and moving forms of Miss Katie and Miss Sue "changed the mail." Indeed, a little later on when mail delivery was organized in town and the post office closed at six, I heard Will Grail say that not all progress was forward and that life in Pine Mills would never be the same without the seven-thirty mail. So long as it lasted, he never failed to attend it.

I don't believe that Lucy had gone to the post office in the evening since Cousin Asa had died, and tonight, especially after what had happened to her yesterday, you could feel the stir she made when she came in. It seemed to make her slender as lace while her eyes stayed brilliant with some

unspoken purpose that would not be denied, and
all the time she stood responding to bows and
respectful greetings, I watched her head lift at
every fresh sound of the door. Then after a suitable interval her eyes would turn to sweep the
latest arrival.

But whoever she looked for did not come. If
it was Will, I had the suspicion he saw her
through the window and gave his key to Jeff
Brady. At any rate, when Jeff opened Will's box,
I saw Lucy twitch her lips as if she were about to
speak to him. At that moment the wickets were
slammed up. Call-box people surged toward the
windows. Jeff slammed the little glass door of
Will's box and slipped out. When I said that we
better go, Lucy obeyed me like a lamb, but all
the way to her house I could feel the faint cloud-
like texture of those invisible cords rising in her.

She paused at the iron gate and I knew she
didn't want me to come in.

"Will you have the tennis court put back by
Saturday, Johnny?" she asked unexpectedly.

"The old tennis court, Lucy!" I protested.
"Why, who would use it?"

"I expect to use it," she said with adamant
sweetness. "Good night." As I made my way

back uptown I thought I could detect her perfume still suspended like a faint but intense trail above the dark sidewalk and it had a heavy, disquieting quality like some deeper, older and more dangerous animal scent.

The old tennis court used to lie somewhat behind the house on the Grail side, but for years had been overgrown with lawn. We had very little time. Lib Fidler hauled clay from the brick pits, and Dick rolled it. I laid down the measurements and ran the broad white lines with a mason's cord and lime. Then Dick set up the posts and painted them white.

Saturday afternoon when I came downtown, Cettie and Lucy were playing singles. Lucy was a picture. In a stiff elaborate white shirtwaist and an old-time white duck skirt to her shoe tops, she glided over the court with erratic dignity. Then she crossed to me on the sidelines and I knew just by the certain feminine way she moved that it was coming now.

"Will you run over for Will and we can play doubles, Johnny?" she asked delicately.

"I haven't any shoes, Lucy," I protested.

"I'm sure we have some in the house that would fit you. There are racquets, too."

"But I don't think Will's supposed to play, Lucy. Doc doesn't want him to."

"In that case I should be the last to let him," she insisted. She stood there just gazing at me, the gray balls held lightly in one hand, her gray eyes without grossness, impurity or imponderable weight and yet with such a disturbing diffused quality that there came to me the words of an old song Lucy's crowd used to sing around the piano:

> There are eyes of blue
> There are brown eyes, too.
> There are eyes of every size and eyes of
>   every hue.
> But I surmise
> That if you are wise
> You'll be careful of the maiden with
>   the dreamy eyes.

"You may remember, Johnny," I heard her go on inflexibly, "the time Will told me I didn't get out of the house enough. You were only a boy. Now he is doing the same, and I want you to tell him I have no intentions of letting him have his way as he let me have mine. If he can't play, he

can sit here on a chair and watch us. The sun will
do him good."

I was not in the habit of calling on Will without an invitation, and even if I had been, I would
have crossed to his house with considerable re-
luctance under the circumstances today. I had
seen him and Polly on the side porch so often that
not until I tapped on the screen door did I realize
it was a French window. But I stood my guns and
knocked the harder when no one answered. Presently Will in a dressing gown, with a look of
faint surprise on his face, raised the upper half,
which was window, opened the lower half,
which was door, unhooked the screen door, and I
found myself in the parlor.

"Sit down, Johnny," he said.

The parlor was lighter and brighter-colored
than the Markles', with chairs and sofas in pale
yellow and gold brocades. There was no piano,
for it was well known that the Grails couldn't
keep a tune in their heads. The room was formal
enough to chill and sober me a little. We talked
about Doc's baseball team, but all the time I felt
he was calmly watching and prepared for me.
When the subject was exhausted, I delivered my
message. His expression never changed.

"Lucy playing tennis?" he asked, although he could have seen her from any one of his north windows.

"Fairly well, too," I nodded.

"Well, she's a bit younger than I. It's a young person's game. Doesn't she know that?"

"Evidently not."

"She better not overdo herself. You know, Lucy isn't a spring chicken any more herself. Now you better not tell her I said so. She never cared for anything vulgar or common."

Rising, he stepped to the French window by which I sat. Turning my head I could look by him and see the court. Lucy's face was toward us, and a lovely face it still was even in that misshapen shirtwaist with a wasp waist and ancient slanting bosom. I glanced up at Will half expecting that he would look as if he had seen a ghost. Instead I was a little shocked. In their youth he and Lucy had seemed nearly of an age. Today his face compared with hers out there looked to be of an older generation, written with the hard story of war, bitterness, and tropical fever. But his eyes were black and undefeated, and I felt that no one, not even Lucy, would ever change them.

"You want something to tell her," he asked. For a minute or so he stood there watching in silence, but I thought I could read what ran behind that forehead, that Lucy could huff and puff but she could never blow his house down; that the tide in their affairs had come and gone, and now she could go to bed at night with those cruel lines from "Maud Muller": "Of all sad words of tongue or pen, the saddest are these: 'It might have been.' "

But when he spoke it was nothing of that.

"Just tell her those days are by for me, Johnny," he said. "Tell her I can't play and I better not sit in the sun. Thank her and say I asked to be excused."

When I came back and delivered his message, Cettie looked a little sorry and shamefaced for Lucy, but she had no need to. Lucy stood so still and light, as if listening to something I couldn't hear. It made me want to let her down painlessly, and Will too, so I told her how old, worn, and ill he looked. I felt that if she could be made to see him in broad daylight with the ravages of his life exposed, it would put a great deal of water under the bridge where it belonged. Certainly no person in her right and reasonable mind, if

Lucy's still was, would hold off her lover all those bright years when he was young and eager for her, and now in his unwilling, anchorite and burned-out years choose to seek him.

But Lucy was hard to understand. The blurred strangeness was suddenly gone from her eyes, and pity stood on her face.

"I had no idea he was ill, Johnny," she cried as if with pain. "This is Mrs. Harter's day off and he probably hasn't had a bite of nourishing food all day." She turned to Cettie. "Will you excuse me? I'll take him something over." Then with her racquet forgotten on the grass, she went into the house.

Chapter Eleven

LEFT soon afterward, but Cettie stayed and told us that on the dot of five o'clock, bathed, combed, and in a fresh monstrosity of an ancient ruffled dress, Lucy had gone across the two lawns with her little brown basket that hadn't been used since old Mrs. Seibert had died. I wondered how much of the food in the snowy napkins and Haviland china had been touched when she came back, but Cettie didn't know. She said she had grown tired of waiting and had come home.

"Perhaps she was still trying to get him to take a bite," I said, remembering the look I had seen in Will's eyes.

"Perhaps," Cettie agreed tranquilly. "And perhaps she found him with a fever and put him to bed."

I saw my mother turn her face quickly away as if to ward off some blow, but what it was I could not imagine. Cettie must have seen it, too.

"What do you think, Mamma?" she asked.

"I don't think much about it," my mother declared sharply. "But if John thinks that Will wouldn't touch the supper after it was prepared and Lucy took it over, I think he's wrong. That would be rude, and Will Grail never was rude. Besides, there are other things he would be much more likely to do under the circumstances."

"What, for instance?" Cettie asked.

"Well," my mother said carefully, "please understand I am not criticizing Lucy for taking his supper over to him. Perhaps I should not have done it, but Lucy was always generous and impulsive. Now the Grails have a great deal of pride. Some people call it stubbornness. I think I would call it gracious stubbornness. Anyhow, if Will was put out at Lucy coming over with his supper, he could simply neglect to pay back the call. In time, I think, that would discourage her from taking it over again."

I had learned to listen to my mother when she spoke about the old families of town and especially of Lucy, for both were of Mattson blood and there was a peculiar affinity between them. It worked out exactly as she said. Cettie reported that Will came no nearer Lucy's house than before, and when she left the basket so he would have to bring it back, he sent it over with Mrs. Harter. So far as I could see, he refrained even from coming out on his side porch that faced the Markle house. It was a favorite spot of his, but the warmest afternoons he stayed inside. As my mother said, Will Grail was one of the most steadfast and dependable of persons, and if something turned you out of his favor, he was exactly the same way against you.

But she was wrong in thinking it would discourage Lucy. Lucy took it with almost holy meekness. Like Tom's death, this was her portion. It brought out that fearful gentleness we knew. She kept on with the little brown basket faithfully as she had to old Mrs. Seibert, and when Will didn't hear or wouldn't answer her tapping on the French window, she would go around to the brass knocker of the great front door, where she made such a pitiful and patient figure that Will did not dare to keep her standing in plain view of everyone. It seemed to give her something just to have visited, seen, and fed him. Once in the Markle house I saw her coming back through the hedge from such a visit. You would have thought from her step that something wonderful had happened, and when she came in the hall, and the light from the stained window fell on her, I thought her face again had the pure, almost pasty quality of a saint's.

Townspeople who missed nothing said it didn't look very nice of Will letting Lucy take him his supper and never knocking on her door in return. They said it was the Oliver case all over again. That was before my time, but the brick Oliver house was still standing and I knew that a Major Beecher had once taken pity on an elderly Miss Oliver living only with an aged brother and had called on her several times to play backgammon. He had also driven her out in a buggy to a country church festival. To his surprise she had taken it seriously, and when he grew alarmed and stayed away, she had spoken to others of their love and began coming over to seek him. In desperation at last he had locked his door by day and kept the house dark by night, and it had affected her mind. She would make her pitiful rounds of town in the evening asking people if they had seen him and looking into any dark buggy on the street to see if he were there.

It was a very uncomfortable story, and I thought it bad enough to have people link Lucy

with the long-departed Miss Oliver. But I had
quite underestimated how much worse it could
be. The first time I heard the rumor I couldn't
believe it. The thing was simply unthinkable. I
said nothing to my mother. I felt sure it must
have reached her ear and Cettie's too, for gossip
travels faster than gospel in Pine Mills. More
than once I saw something deep and troubled in
my mother's eyes, but I knew that neither she
nor Cettie would bring up such a thing about our
cousin, and neither would I.

Then one evening at supper my mother said
that old Mrs. Grail had sent for her, and she
wanted me to go along. Without another word, I
knew what was coming and that my mother
wished me to stand with her against the old
woman.

Old Lady Grail, as we called her, lived in
the large stone house on the terrace. Today they
would cut such a knoll down to the level of the
street, but in those days to have your house a little higher than others' was thought to give it dis-
tinction. No neighbor could look into your upstairs windows, but you could look down on the
town. The old Grail house commanded especially a view of the depot with the arrival and de-

parture of trains, and when I was a small boy I tangled it in my mind with far places and world commerce.

Tonight we climbed the two long flights of stone steps to the veranda, where my mother stood gathering herself and breath before ringing the bell. This was the coolest porch in town and perhaps the most spacious, running the full front of the house, but almost never was it used, not even on the hottest evenings. The scrolled woodwork on the porch had a conservative look in its oyster-colored paint, and the wide hall and great parlor inside struck me as formal and bare. However, the maid took us up to the sitting room on the second floor, a room carpeted, cushioned and stuffed with a plethora of furnishings.

Will's grandmother greeted us with a plush smile and pious nod from her chair. She was still stoutish at ninety, a woman who seemed to have just drawn her breath in and her bosom out, which gave her a powerful, restrained, and secretive look. She was plainly the head of her clan, and the eyes in her padded and endlessly cross-wrinkled cheeks were black and hard as polished beads. You could easily tell where Will had got his eyes.

She and my mother talked harmless women's
things for a while. Then her daughter, Mrs.
Pumphry, who lived with her, came in, and the
same thing went pointlessly on. Finally my
mother took hold of the gloves on her lap, a sig-
nal that she was about to go. Mrs. Pumphry sub-
sided like a small girl who has been talking too
much, and looked at her mother.

"Matty," the old lady said at once, her voice
harsh as a parrot's, "what's all this bad talk I hear
about your Lucy?"

I had to admire the way my mother held herself without flinching. "Just about Lucy?" she
asked quietly.

"You know about it then. Well, of course,
Will is mixed up in it, too. But as I hear, it's not
his doings. I think it was nice of Lucy taking his
supper over to him sometimes, although she
didn't have to. Will knows he's always welcome
at my table. But she oughtn't to go farther than
that, Matty."

"No, she oughtn't to, and I'm sure she
doesn't," my mother said firmly and cooly.
"Lucy was never that kind of girl."

"Well, I didn't think she was a fast woman
either. But she's been acting very queer of late.

Still she's not that queer not to know that people will talk if they see her doing anything she shouldn't."

"What people?" my mother asked bitterly. "The kind of people who have been up all night at the Legion drinking?"

"Well," old Mrs. Grail cried, "that wouldn't stop them from seeing what they hadn't ought to see at two o'clock in the morning."

"And what's that?" my mother asked, her face white. "Whatever it is, I don't believe it for a number of reasons. Will doesn't care for Lucy any more in the old way, and hasn't for several years, I am sure. He never calls at her house to see her. If he is so particular and exclusive, he could easily lock the side screen door and keep any undesirable person out."

"He could," the old lady agreed. "But he's a man!" She gave me an owlish and withering look as if to say: So much for you, young man.

My mother did not continue the argument. She stood up. I had seldom seen her so aroused underneath, but then slandering Lucy was the same as slandering Cettie or me.

"I really have to go."

"Now, Matty," the old lady placated, "don't

get mad at me. You're the only one I have to talk to. I thought you and I ought to do something. We don't want our children forgetting their poor fathers' and mothers' good names. I thought maybe you would talk to Lucy."

"Have you talked to Will?"

"No, but I would have if he wasn't so touchy. He'd never come around again."

"If you can't speak to Will," my mother told her coldly, "I couldn't possibly bring up such outrageous lying gossip to Lucy. Good night."

Mrs. Pumphry hurried anxiously down to let us out herself, but my mother didn't give her any satisfaction at the door. Her feet went fast and she didn't say a word all the way home. As I expected, Cettie had stayed up to hear all about it. She looked up eagerly as we came in, but my mother went right into the dining room and kitchen. We could hear her picking up things and setting them away.

"Of course, there's not a vestige of truth in it," she declared, coming suddenly back to the room. "Just the same, I thought it best to tell Lucy some time ago that people were watching and talking. If there *had* been even the slightest indiscretion, that would have stopped it." She put

Cettie's hat away in the hall closet and reappeared at the door. "I like to be friendly with my neighbors. But I should like to have told Tilly Grail that even if this terrible gossip had been true, which of course it isn't, it wouldn't be the first time such a thing happened in this town, and she would know exactly what I meant." Then my mother went determinedly upstairs.

Now what unknown scandal did that raise from the dead? I did not look at Cettie. I still couldn't believe this thing about our Lucy. Taking my hat, I went outside and turned down to the railroad. It was extraordinarily still and peaceful there. Not a soul moved, nor a wheel turned. Only the blue and red switch-lights sent their pure colors through the night. It always seemed curious to see them still lighted at this hour, for the last train was in long ago and there wouldn't be another till early morning. The freight house looked strangely deserted with its great doors closed. The weigh station was dark and the depot silent. Not even the telegraph instrument moved. The only sound between the Pottsville Street and Mill Street crossings was that of water running over the slimy sides of the water tower.

I think I knew where I was going from the

first, down through the cut where my eyes could hardly find the ties and my feet took the cinder path, then up the cross street that came down to the rails, and back to Swatara Street at the Lutheran Church hill where the quieter part of town stood hushed and hidden behind the great dark bulk of the trees. Even the occasional street lights were lost in the endless foliage. But as I came upon the level I could see light ahead in Will Grail's library. The yellow blinds were down. I stood there watching for a little, but not a shadow fell on the golden squares. I could imagine Will sitting there alone with his slippered feet on a hassock reading one of his three evening papers, the *Philadelphia Bulletin*, the *Harrisburg Telegraph* and the *Miners' Journal*.

Just the same, it made me uneasy to see Lucy's big house beyond looking dim in contrast. There was a faint light from the glass above and beside the big front door and from Mary's and Regina's rooms on the third floor rear. No more, and that gave me pause. I wondered where Lucy could be tonight. Then when I reached the other side I could see all the windows of her bedroom alight. They were a shining pastel green in the night, and knowing her room so well, I could almost see her up there, in negligee, brushing her hair or sitting gracefully at the massive mahogany desk whose writing board folded back and whose ink-spotted brass chains tugged and groaned at the lightest touch like a drawbridge.

I was about to go on when I heard a stirring in the shrubbery. I stepped through the black iron gate and around to the deep shadow between the two yards, a hydrangea hedge famous through the countryside and when in bloom a sight to see, with all the great pale heads tinged with pink. But tonight it was a long black blot.

"Come out of that," I said, as low and sternly as I could. "Or I'll turn the hose on you."

There was hasty whispering, and three dark boyish forms crawled out. I didn't know a mother's son of them in the gloom until I shook them one after the other by the shoulder and made them talk. They were all in high school and stammered they had been looking for a ball they had lost in the hedge.

"Don't expect me to believe that," I said. "I know what you were after. Now go on home and go to bed. You can tell anybody who asks you that you didn't see a thing and it's a pack of lies."

I stayed very little longer myself. I didn't

want anybody to come along and say that I had
been there watching, too. It gave me a better
feeling to leave with Lucy's bedroom windows
alight. But that night a curious thing happened.

My room at home was on the north side
of the house and fronted on Swatara Street. I
didn't sleep very well, awoke chilly, and got
up to find more cover. As I rose I glimpsed
through the front window a man's figure
coming up the opposite side of the street.
There was a street light on the corner and he
looked familiar, a stocky, impressive, middle-
aged man, bareheaded but otherwise very well
dressed. What drew my attention was the peculiar way he walked, leaning somewhat forward
as if in pain or difficulty. As I turned away from
the window, the utter silence seemed peculiar,
and I looked back. He was still moving up the
sidewalk. The night was perfectly still and
damp, and I couldn't understand how his feet
made no sound on the bricks. I believed I could
have heard a leaf drop. Then back in bed again
it came to me whom he looked like. It was Cousin
Asa, and that troubled me so that I had barely
fallen asleep an hour or so later when the fire
gong woke me.

We have today what is known as a siren in Pine
Mills, but then the town had a great iron hoop
hung in the open belfry of the hose house. A
clapper was connected to this by means of a rope
to the engine room downstairs. The first man to
run to the hose house looked at the chart on the
wall and then pulled the rope the number of
times required for the location, repeating it after
suitable pauses until enough men had come to
take out the engine. Today the siren is used for
various occasions, including celebrations, and
even when blown for a fire has, I think, a rather
cheerful appeal. But the clang of the iron hoop
had a deep sinister sound and could be fittingly
used for nothing but a fire, when it struck terror
in the heart just to hear it.

I lay in bed counting the strokes. It sounded
like the Methodist Church hill. My mother was
at Cousin Henry's in Hazleton, and when I went
into her room I could see an ominous red mound
in the sky. It seemed to be directly down Swatara
Street. When I got outside, men and boys were
running on the street, while women in bathrobes
and kimonos stood in doorways or pulled on
clothing at windows, from where they called to
ask where the fire was.

"It's at Markles'!" I heard someone answer, and so indeed it looked to me, even from the old tannery. But when I reached the Methodist Church hill where the street curved a little, I was relieved to see the great bulk of Lucy's house outlined blackly against the flames. Then I knew it must be the Pinchers' house on the side street. When I went through Lucy's yard I could smell the burning pine. A strong east wind was blowing from Birds Hill sending the great black and orange flames across the alley to lick at Will Grail's stable.

"Where's Miss Lucy?" I called to old Mary and Regina, who stood strangely at their back door.

To my surprise, they didn't answer, only stared at me frightened, and I went over to Will Grail's yard. There always has been something about a fire in Pine Mills that deeply shakes us natives. I think it is the sight of incredible flames lighting up peaceful houses and trees we know so well so that the most familiar neighborhood becomes a strange and terrifying scene. Glancing around I could hardly believe that these were Lucy's and Will's houses or that back there was Swatara Street with the Hickory House and

Bradley's store. Everything looked changed and hideous in the red glare and pouring black smoke and with the hoarse shouts of firemen, who tonight seemed like nobody we knew.

It was strange, I thought, that neither Lucy nor Will had come out, especially the latter, for his stable was already caught up with flames. Nearly everybody else in town had come or was in the process of arrival. I saw people from North Pine Mills and Chickentown, who had never dared to enter Lucy's or Will's gates before, push through and swarm over both lawns, stretching along the hedge out of line of the driving smoke which made the side street untenable.

Where the hell was Will, I asked myself, for sparks and brands were raining now on the shingle roof of his house. But the only sign of life about the house was a light burning quietly and calmly in his front corner bedroom upstairs, as if anyone needed light at a time like this. Firemen were running around the house.

"How do you get in this place, Johnny?" Hotz Moyer yelled at me. "Every damned door's locked."

I told him I thought I could get in and took him to the side porch. Already I had seen him swing the screen door and knew that its hook must have hung unfastened tonight. Now I showed him how to lift the French window and push back the lower doors. There was light in the parlor from the hall, and I led the way in.

"Will!" I called.

After the lurid confusion without, the house inside seemed extraordinarily peaceful and composed, with every chair in the parlor in its dignified place, and out in the hall the white woodwork soft in the chandelier's light.

"Hey, Colonel!" Hotz shouted. "You still in bed?"

He started up the stairs for the attic, then drew back abashed. I stared. A delicate figure, almost an apparition, was coming down. In a simple nightdress and silken dressing gown, it looked like a girl, but a woman's hair had been piled on her head. Freed of stays and those ancient outlandish clothes, she looked more slender than I had ever seen her. A man's coat had been thrown over her shoulders, but it couldn't conceal the fragile identity of Lucy Markle.

Right behind her came Will, tall, fully dressed, his old face mottled, his back stiff, his eyes pitch-black and unreadable.

"Take Lucy over, Johnny," he said to me, hard and short, then turned to the speechless fireman and asked what he could do.

If there was ever a task in the world I hated, it was to take Lucy out into the pitiless glare and crowd. Only Lucy didn't seem to mind or think it anything at all. Her arm in mine was weightless, and her step as in a dream. As we walked out on the porch through the French window, the light seemed blinding. I did not look around, but I could feel the hush of the townspeople, and at every step I imagined the eyes of Old Lady Grail fixed on us, triumphantly staring. Even the firemen at their hoses were silent. My only consolation was that my mother wasn't there. As we reached the hedge, the roof of Will's stable fell in.

I took Lucy to her side steps.

"You needn't come any farther, Johnny. I can get in. I left the door open," she told me quietly, and vanished.

Chapter Twelve

My mother came home on the train next day, pleaded a headache and went straight to bed. She would see no one. That afternoon we heard that Will was packing up to visit Canadian friends with whom he had fought in the opening years of the war. But Lucy remained in Pine Mills and came out on the street that day as lightly as ever. Indeed, we hadn't seen her so floating and radiant for a long time. It was as if last night's affair had only given her a sense of the security she had been denied so long, had restored her place in Will's life and affection and demonstrated it to the whole town.

She told Cettie she wanted her and her mother to come to the house Saturday evening, whispering that it would be a formal dinner to announce her coming marriage to Will. They were to be wed next June. Cettie said that, knowing all that had gone before, she was a tiny bit startled and embarrassed, but she had no need to be. Lucy was exquisitely at ease. You might have thought, Cettie said, that this was the first time she had ever been promised and that everything had been wholly proper and aboveboard.

My mother got out of bed when Cettie told her. We felt her approval of Lucy acting so swiftly, that it lessened in some degree the breach, for it gave the impression that Lucy and Will had been closer than people thought, might really have been promised beforehand, which allowed some small excuse for their transgression. Mother even confided to us now the dialogue between her and the close-mouthed Charley Fisher on the way home. Someone had told her in Pottsville about the fire, but she had not believed what she heard.

Then on the train home she had run into Charley.

"Any news in Pine Mills since I'm away?"

"No, ma'am. Nothing particular," Charley told her.

"Wasn't there a fire or something?" my mother persisted.

"We did have a fire, but it wasn't much account," Charley said.

"They said Pinchers' house burned down."

"Yes, ma'am, but you know nobody lived in it."

"Didn't Will Grail's stable burn down, too?"

"Well, yes, it did, but he didn't have anything in it either but trash."

"I heard," my mother went on, "that the firemen found someone in Will's house when his roof caught on fire. Is that true, Charley?"

"Well, it's supposed to be true," Charley admitted reluctantly.

"And she came right out in front of everybody?"

"I believe."

"Who was it?"

"I don't know as I heard exactly."

"Charley. Was it a relative of mine?"

He looked grave.

"So they say, Miss Matty."

"You were there and saw it yourself, Charley?"

He just kept looking down at the floor, and by that my mother knew it must be so.

It put us into a better humor to have our mother tell us, but I didn't like the shocked talk among the townspeople. I drove Cettie and my mother down to the dinner. It seemed very gay when we got there, with Cousin Lucy's house brilliantly lighted and cars parked one after the other along the curb. I ran around to the kitchen, where waves of fragrant vapors met me at the door. Regina had a woman to help her in the kitchen and so had Mary in the dining room. The long table ran almost from wall to wall, loaded with china, silver, and glass while a row of tall pink candles stood ready to burn. Pasteboard boxes tied with white ribbon were set at each place and Mary showed me what was inside one of them, a pink confection that looked something like Cousin Asa's brick church. Even the steeple of white icing was there, considerably shortened and looking good enough to eat. Tiny sugar roses climbed over the church door, in front of which stood the miniature figures of a bride and groom, one bearing a card lettered Lucy and the other, Will.

My mother said when she came home that Will's going away had rather spoiled the dinner for her, and it also had been a little elaborate and flowery after all that had happened before. But she and Cettie had only praise for Lucy herself. They said you wouldn't have guessed there was

anything wrong from the way she sat there ut-
terly happy at the head of the table in the huge
old dining room, creating a glow of light and
warmth that spread over the guests and over the
snowy cloth and Mary's freshly polished silver
until the candles sparkling on Cousin Ruby's
two-dozen set of gold-band china seemed to shed
their soft fire back into another day and on another and younger Mary hovering around the
table. And back on another and younger Lucy,
too. They said something had happened to her.
They knew it the moment they saw her in an
evening dress, something she hadn't worn for
many years. It was only an old red one, but Miss
Sally had worked over it, and evening dresses
hadn't changed much the last years anyway.
They were still about as long as they always were.
Anyhow in that dress and low slippers Lucy
seemed as perfectly normal as anybody there and
as she hadn't been since her father had died in
the mine. It was as if she had just woke up from
a long and clouded sleep. She had even made
fun of her ancient wardrobe and told everybody
that next week she was going to New York to get
some new clothes and incidentally order her
trousseau, and that Cettie was going along.

A little skeptical, we waited to see what would happen. Then Tuesday I took them and their bags in my car to the train before going to the colliery. At the station, with everyone looking up to Lucy, with Frank Dietz chatting through the ticket window while he nimbly plied his telegraph instrument and, when the train came in, with the conductor, brakeman, and Frank all helping Lucy and Cettie aboard with the luggage, it seemed that a bit of the rich old-time Markle days had returned. Cettie wrote home that at Auburn, where they changed trains, they had taken the parlor car and that the ancient porter had asked if this wasn't Miss Lucy and had spoken of her mother and father. When they arrived at the Waldorf, the old Waldorf where Cousin Asa and Cousin Ruby always used to stay, the clerk called one of the managers who remembered Lucy and welcomed her. Each of them had her own bedroom overlooking Fifth Avenue, and on the table when they got in was a bouquet of flowers. But more than New York or the trip, Cettie wrote, was the continued change in Lucy. She had never known her like this before, nor would we if we saw her in Peacock Alley or at the theater and supper clubs, as Lucy still called them.

When we saw her again in Pine Mills, we knew what Cettie meant, for Lucy's face was like many years ago. She stepped down off the train slim and modern in an exquisite suit that looked like Paris. Her skirts were shorter than anyone in Pine Mills at that day dared. What in heaven's name, I thought, had made her keep those legs covered all these years when any woman her age would have sold her soul for such a youthful and shapely pair to show to advantage. An unquenchable flame seemed lighted in her, and yet as Lucy chatted to us and waited for her and Cettie's truckload of bags and boxes to be unloaded, I saw her keep scanning the little crowd of onlookers as if she didn't know that Will was still away and had hoped that he would meet her. It gave me the peculiar uneasy feeling of having lived through this scene before.

In October we heard that John Trumbo, our Pine Mills plumber, was blowing the water from the pipes in Will Grail's house and that Will had not come back to Pine Mills at all but had gone south for the winter. It startled us. At supper that evening Cettie confessed that Lucy had written Will every day they were in New York and she had not seen her get a letter from him in return.

"Has something happened to their affair?" she wanted to know.

"Something happened long ago, Cettie," my mother said gravely.

"But everything was all right," Cettie cried.

"We don't know. We only heard one side."

"But you always hear it from the bride, and Lucy is perfectly normal and fine."

"That's true," my mother said, ever scrupulous and fair. She was silent a moment. "But we must remember she was also perfectly normal and fine when Tom was killed."

Cettie and I sat there sobered. What Cettie thought I do not know, but a number of questions came forward from where they had lain uneasily in the back of my mind. More than once I had asked myself was it possible that Lucy had taken marriage for granted after what had happened at the fire? Could it be that Will had never been consulted, but only informed? It would explain many things — his clearing out so quickly, even before the roof of his house had been fixed, and his grim silence in the mails. But what in the devil's name would come out of it if Lucy kept on with this pretty business that wasn't so?

As weeks went by, the townspeople began to talk. They thought it very strange that a man soon to be married took pains to go away so far from his bride. And they thought it stranger, when Will came back to open his house in April, that a bridal couple living next door to each other was never seen out in each other's company. In New York Lucy had ordered a Pierce-Arrow car, and when it came, Fred Jones, who had driven Cousin Asa back and forth to the colliery in the red Rambler, took her out the Pleasant Valley road and showed her how to start and stop and change gears. Old Jack Hooker, who had owned the first garage in Pine Mills, said a lady had no business at a steering wheel and predicted that Miss Lucy would end in the ditch. Just the same, in a week she was expertly raising great clouds of dust through the countryside, and the next day you would see old Dick washing the machine on the drive, where it would stand with its royal blue enamel and bright nickel plate dancing in the sun. Doc said he thought the car would do Will's health a lot of good and that Lucy would make him a first-rate chauffeur. But

if Will ever went out in it, I never heard of anyone who saw him.

Old Mrs. Gruver of Back Street, who had seen
a great deal in the long space of time measured
by her one remaining tooth, said:

"Now just wait. They're not married yet.
I've seen them closer than this before. When I
hear the preacher say Amen, then I'll believe it.
Those two never had any luck together. It's not
their fault. Nobody can put together what wasn't
meant to be."

Just the same, Lucy went right ahead with
her plans of remodeling the big house for the
wedding. She had workmen sawing, pounding,
and pulling things to pieces till my mother said
that Cousin Asa and Cousin Ruby must have
turned over in their graves. She had the golden
oak pillars torn out, the tall mirrors cut down in
the parlor, and the palms, ferns, and rubber
plants thrown out of the conservatory, which
she modernized into a sun porch. Corners of
bedrooms were walled up for baths, and the old
fixtures of present bathrooms ripped out for
shiny luxurious new ones. The dangerous and
smelly carbide plant was thrown out, the house
wired, then wires and useless carbide pipes alike

plastered over and brighter paper laid on the walls.

I think it was Lucy's sheer confidence and happiness that encouraged us and carried us to the end. She seemed so capable, acted as if she knew thoroughly what she was about. She told us what Will would wear for the wedding. We saw her take him his supper on Mrs. Harter's afternoon off and run over otherwise on occasion. Cettie helped her address and mail the engraved invitations which went to Will's people and friends as well as Lucy's. And the wedding presents, when they came, gave an appearance of solid reality, that everything must be all right.

How many there were who felt that there was still something very radically wrong, I don't know, but the day of the wedding I'd have given a great deal to have been a thousand miles away. The day broke clear and still in Pine Mills, with every house and tree standing distinct and motionless among its fellows, reminding me of that first unhappy day which had been the cause of all the trouble, the day I had run the message of Tom's death to Lucy and her father. With her father long since gone now, she had asked me to give her away. Cettie was to be maid of honor, and Will's friend, Joe Donahue of Pottsville, best man.

We were all to meet at her house and go to church together. It was already a little late when Cettie and I arrived. I ran in and found Joe Donahue in the library. He gave me the first real shred of assurance. Then we heard a door open upstairs and Mary's and other voices. Presently Lucy appeared at the head of the stairs. Her wedding dress, although only a few had actually seen it, was already by hearsay the talk of the women of town. She had declined, I knew, to wear a stitch of her Grandmother Markle's lace from the other and unlucky gown. Seeing her in creamy silk and satin, taller than I knew her, she seemed like a vision from Joe Donahue's Catholic Church, but it was her face that held me, the gentle, virgin, almost perishable face of a creature who had spent her life in a convent screened from men and who now with the spiritual peace of that life still around her was about to enter the world of the flesh and the devil.

She greeted me in the delicate way she always had in church. Almost at once Joe Donahue came out of the library. Finally Cettie ran in to see why we weren't coming. No one mentioned

Will's name, but I knew it lay heavily on all our minds and hearts as we stood there waiting together, the only sound that of the clocks of the library and parlor mingling. Twice Mary, who was there too, with her hand on the doorknob ready to let the bridegroom in and us out, moved to the parlor window, and I thought her face was grimmer when she returned.

"How soon's Will coming?" I couldn't help asking Joe at last.

"He didn't say," the best man stammered. "He just told me not to wait for him. So I came over. Is anything wrong?" he asked, looking from face to face.

A little cold chill had reached up my spine, and in that moment I knew almost to a certainty that Will wasn't coming, that he had probably never promised or intended to come, and that's why he had sent Joe over, so his friend wouldn't know and couldn't share in the blame. I looked at Cettie. She wouldn't look at me. Her eyes were fastened on the hands of the clock on the library mantel, but through the back hall I had a glimpse of Regina, and her face was thoroughly frightened. I peered up the hall stairs. Although the banister's finish had been changed, it looked much the same. I could see the very crook where Lucy long ago had inclined her lovely young head and then turned back, and the place had an ominous air to me today. But Lucy never saw it. She stood there so light as if in a cloud, and as the seconds ticked on I thought I could feel those silken filaments once more rising and tightening in her.

"You and Cettie and I will start," she told me softly.

"But, Lucy — " I protested.

"We'll go in one car. Joe, you can bring Will in the other when he comes," she said.

I tried to hold her back by the arm, but she had that terrible gentleness I had seen before and there was no stopping her. She was calling Will's hand, I knew, and she intended to see it through. If he dishonored her, he would have to do it in front of everybody, for she would fulfill her part to the very aisle of the church. Lifting her train, she moved to the door. Mary reluctantly opened it, and Lucy led the way across the porch, holding her skirts with all her old-time dignity, moving slowly and firmly through the gate and into the first car. Shaking a little inside, Cettie and I followed.

A score or more of women and children together with a few town characters such as Eddie
Carr had collected around the church steps waiting for the bride to come, and as she passed
through she smiled to them faintly and to the
rest of the wedding party waiting anxiously in
the vestibule. I could see as we came in that the
church was packed. Filled chairs stood at the
sides and rear. Lucy had been bound this time to
have everything she had missed before, the
month of June, a big church wedding and guests
who should rise when the bride entered and stand
throughout the ceremony. They had been thoroughly instructed and now, as it was already past
noon, some, looking back and seeing her there,
began to rise until the entire gathering of company stood. I felt myself start to sweat. Never
had I seen Cettie's face so white. But Lucy gave
no sign.

More than once Cettie and I have hoped that
never may we have to suffer again what we went
through that day. As I said before, we were late
and the minister, seeing us coming, unable to
conceive of a missing bridegroom and confused
perhaps by the rising of the people, had gone
hurriedly up the aisle to the altar, where he

turned with sudden solemnity and stood ready to
receive the wedding party. But no such procession came to him. Minute after minute he stood
there waiting, at first puzzled, then uncomfortable and disturbed but bearing it in true martyr
fashion and continuing to stand, his eyes fixed on
the bride at the rear as if for some explanation of
this dilemma and clue for him to follow.

But Lucy could give him no help. She stood a
little apart from us as if alone against all this
company and the world. I never saw her so fragile and defenseless, and as the restlessness and
embarrassment among the people grew, I began
to pity her. It was true that once upon a time she
had done this same thing to Will, and perhaps
she had it coming to her, but after twenty endless
minutes I felt that she had fully paid for it, and
now as she stood there so helpless and exposed to
all the shame and humiliation that would follow, no one could help feeling terribly sorry for
her. More than once I leaned toward her and
under my breath begged her to give up and go,
or how in God's name was this to end, but she
pretended not to hear me.

At exactly twelve thirty there was the sound
of a car stopping outside, and Will and Joe came

in. No one would have guessed from Will's un-
hurried manner that anything was wrong. He
had had his say. He would not throw Lucy to the
wolves, but he had given notice to all concerned
that he was going into this against his will. Perhaps he had so planned it from the beginning,
and from his point of view I could understand it
perfectly, but I wondered if he had any notion
that a woman, and especially Lucy, could forgive it. Indeed now that he had come, I should
not have been surprised to see her turn quietly
and leave him. And if she stayed, I fully expected
her to go through the ceremony with an icy,
wounded pride that would chill most of us to the
bone and leave us praying that God help them
afterward.

Instead, Lucy lifted her head and gave him
the purest look, one of ethereal and eternal devo-
tion, and I saw his black eyes change. For a moment or two he gazed on her with a strange scru-
tiny, I thought, and respect. Then with the
organ suddenly sounding and filling the church
with a kind of audible joy, he and Joe Donahue
gravely matched steps to march down the aisle.
All through the ceremony he stood by her side
soldierly and attentive, and as their vows rang

out in the hushed church, I felt that these two had gone through a great deal and had nearly succeeded in wrecking each other's life, but that it was going to be all right at last. At the end when he turned and kissed her with apparent affection in front of us all, I saw many who watched and knew the whole story wipe their eyes.

I had seen the Markle house crowded in the old days, but seldom as it was for the wedding reception. Autos were parked from beyond the Methodist Church to Boyers' corner on both sides of the street, and the caterers' darkies from Philadelphia, some of whom had been here for the other less happy occasion, outdid themselves with smiling faces. There were lobster salad, breast of chicken, sliced Virginia baked ham, fancy sandwiches by the bushel basket, all kinds of creams and ices, a great tiered wedding cake in addition to the several hundred tiny cake portions to be taken home as mementos in their small ivory boxes tied with white satin ribbon. Wines flowed, despite the prohibitionists who turned their glasses down at the table. When Will and Lucy left, rice rained like sleet, and as the car started, a string of cowbells that some of the yokelry of town had tied under the axle during the reception began to make a deafening but pleasant revelry. Crowding the sidewalk and great triangular porch, the guests could hear the happy sound as far off as Pottsville Street.

Chapter Thirteen

Lucy and Will spent the summer honey-mooning in Maine. Her letters back to us were light as butterfly tracings, just a few ecstatic words with a sprig of fragrant balsam or birch bark or painted trillium pressed within, but they had the knack of imprisoning a fragment of her spirit and transporting it through trains, mail clerks and date stamps unharmed so that when you opened the envelope, there she was, just a bit and snatch of her, but unmistakable in the gay words, the artistic stroke of the pen and the faint fragrance of the flower. Indeed, when I still smell a balsam pillow I can see Lucy in my mind floating through the dim aisles of the North Woods or sitting on a green bed of moss with Will's head in her lap.

There were several more changes she wrote me she wanted in the house, and it was August before all was ready. I saw to the last details myself and wired that their house was waiting for them, but they did not arrive. The town was eager to see the married pair, and most every day someone or other asked when they were coming home. Then in September we had sudden word that they were boarding ship in Boston for Italy. The telegram was written in the same extravagant words as the letters, but we thought it strange that, if they had to go, Will and Lucy could not have sailed from New York and run over to Pine Mills first.

From then on we had only picture postcards dashed off in Lucy's hand, as though a round of pleasures on foreign soil did not leave her more that a moment in which to remember us. So far as we knew, they stayed in Italy all winter. The day in February my mother died we received from her hand a colored postcard of a fabulous white beach lined with tropical green palms. In Pine Mills we had to shovel through two feet of snow to dig the grave, and while we stood on the snowy waste with an icy wind blowing and the bitter sound of the pick in the frozen ground, I could see in my mind Lucy and Will lazily swimming in the soft blue warm Mediterranean Sea.

Lucy and Will stayed on in Europe. When

townspeople kept asking why they didn't come home, we said they were having a marvelous time, that Lucy was happy as a lark, and people said they were glad the honeymoon lasted so long. But privately we thought it strange we had no letter from Lucy even about our mother's death, just these bright postcards dashed off in her aristocratic light blue ink. They peculiarly angered Cettie. She said that now that Lucy had Will, she was showing her selfish streak again, that she always wanted everything and gave nothing, and as far as she, Cettie, was concerned, she wouldn't write her another line.

Next spring we found that Lucy had disposed of the Kalmia Colliery to the Reading Coal and Iron Company, and that George Mansfield of Cousin Asa's old Pottsville bank was personally looking after Lucy's affairs. Every month he mailed Mary and Regina their checks, and a third to cover food and miscellany. They had nothing to do but live in the big house and see that moths, frost and rain did not get in. I thought it sadder than ever now to pass the two lonely old houses, one long since closed, dark, the water blown from its plumbing; the other newer-looking, painted, renovated but closed too, except for the two old servants living in the rear like mice in their nests in a granary.

All this time the picture postcards trickled in with their quaint sights and funny-looking foreign stamps. I remember Capri, the red roofs of Bandol, Mentone, a shrine in the Tyrol, the backs of the great Alps, a balcony in Taormina, the Blue Grotto from Naples, scenes from American battlefields in France, including "Aviator Quentin Roosevelt's Grave." Sometimes the cards were reproductions of French or Italian paintings, or of places like the Reims Cathedral, and San Marco in Venice or the Grand Canal. Often they were scenes of places famous for their baths like Karlsbad, Baden and Aix-les-Bains. Always the crosses on Lucy's *t*'s kept flying like pennants, yet only twice was the message of any length. Once she raved about a fabulous little hotel they had found, of white walls with light blue shutters. It stood far out on a point in the blue Mediterranean and overlooked the monastery of Amalfi. And the other time she told how she and Will were daily showered with roses and orange blossoms by a hotel man in Sorrento who used to be a waiter at Kugler's in Philadelphia.

Lucy didn't write often, but in five or six years

a lot of postcards can pile up. I came on them just the other day in the attic, tied with a red cord. The sight of their peculiar foreign style and colors brought back Lucy as I used to fancy her when a card came, flitting and twinkling among the palaces of Europe, the same delicate and lovely cousin untouched by the passage of time. I doubted then if we should ever see her in our beloved Pennsylvania again.

Of all the months of the year to an exile, April in our country holds the tenderest pull I know, for I have been an exile myself, and it was a day in April that Lucy returned to Pine Mills. I had been to a convention of coal men at Philadelphia, and as I neared home all I thought of were the newly green meadows I knew so well along the road and the ground under the spring plowing, not the dull clods turned up by the plow in November, but a rich chocolate soil, living and warm. When I reached town I found that the great trees along Swatara Street had shoved out in my absence and formed a continuous arching bower of greenery. As I passed Cemetery Hill, I glanced up and saw two women on our family lot. In a moment I had stopped the car and backed up to where I could see again. They

seemed to be standing by my mother's grave. One
of them was old Mary. The other held a handkerchief to her eyes. I didn't remember ever seeing her before. Then as my car climbed the hill,
I saw that it was Lucy.

There was a shock in recognizing her, especially up here, that I had not foreseen. She wore
an exquisitely tailored green suit, and a hat with
a mist of green feather. Even her shoes had the
unmistakable Paris stamp. She still had that upward, alive carriage, but the fragile and gossamer lightness had fled. As I got out of the car, I
realized she looked stocky like her father. The
slender throat had coarsened, and the once delicate cheeks salted and strewn with countless
faint wrinkles. But the sharpest insult, almost
sacrilege, was something I had seen only on old
women before, a kind of sagging protuberance
at the bottom of either cheek, as if the muscles
there had enlarged and hardened from too frequent setting of the jaw until it gave the face a
look of ancient and bitter disappointment.

She quickly wiped her eyes when she saw me,
tried to throw everything off and be her old self
again. She kissed me and we talked of Cettie and
her baby until presently I drove her and Mary

back to the house. It was good to see blue wood smoke rising from the Markle chimney, the shades up and the large windows free.

When we got out I asked what I had been wanting to ask ever since I knew it was Lucy, but something had restrained me.

"How's Will?"

By the suddenly hard, almost cruel expression on old Mary's face, I knew that I had probed to a vital spot.

"He's fine as can be expected," Lucy said quickly.

I stepped ahead to open the gate and then the door for her.

"You there, my dear?" Lucy called up the stairs in a high soprano. "I've brought somebody to see you, Will. An old friend!"

There was no answer.

"Sit down a few minutes, Johnny," she said lightly, and ran up the stairs, while I went in the library and let myself into one of the leather chairs that hadn't felt my body in half a decade.

I expected them to come down together and was surprised when Lucy called me to come up. I found her smiling brightly but fixedly at me from the head of the stairs, as if she didn't quite

see me at all. She took me into the front bedroom
that had been her father's, where a wheel chair
was drawn up with its back toward one of the
side windows. I had the feeling that it had lately
been turned the other way for the occupant to
sit there looking at Will Grail's old fieldstone
house next door. But could this be Will, I asked
myself. There was no other person but Lucy and
me in the room, and yet I didn't see how it could
be. The body looked crippled and shrunken as if
by more powerful acids than gentle age. The
head turned faintly toward where I stood just inside the door, but it didn't turn far enough, and I
knew that this was as far as the head could move.

Skillfully Lucy wheeled the chair around,
just a foot or more, but it was far enough to let
him see me. I saw then that the dark eyes were
deeply sunken among the bones. Those eyes were
the only part of him that looked familiar. Their
black depths were unchanged. They gave me a
look that said something. What it was I did not
know at the time, but I thought I could feel why
Lucy had cried so bitterly at the grave of my silent mother, who had once tried so gently and
vainly to help her.

He made no attempt to rise, and I knew he had

173

been used to sitting like that for a long time. I felt
foolish when I lifted his helpless hand, and he
did not make it any easier for me. After the first
greeting he did not talk, just sat there like a
burnt-out ember that continued faintly to glow
and fade not because of any substance left within
it to burn but from the reflected fire of a live coal
close beside it. Lucy and I worked to keep the
conversation going. She kept bringing him into
the talk as a mother does her child who is present,
a big boy who refuses to speak for himself. Only
once while I was there did she treat him as a
normal grownup. That was when his eyes slowly
met mine.

"Well, how's the Tom Grail Post getting
along?"

"Don't speak that name!" Lucy turned on
him, her eyes blazing. She added bitterly: "And
to think that once I pitied him!"

Now what did she mean by that, I wondered.
What she said embarrassed me, but Will's black
eyes remained unchanged. He must have heard it
often before. I made up my mind to go very soon,
but Lucy was saying that for Will's sake I must
stay to supper — dinner she called it now. Her

eyes insisted. Will's said nothing. I couldn't go
and I couldn't very well stay, but I had to do one
or the other.

It was the old house and room that finally got
me, I think, the familiar and beloved old house
and this room with the remembered painting of
St. Anthony's Wilderness on the wall, with
Cousin Asa and Cousin Ruby in silver frames
on the bureau, and the great walnut bed we
called the Mormon bed because it was wide
enough for a man and his wives. Now Lucy
for the first time had brought home her husband to this house and bed. Once the French
nurse wheeled him away but only for a little,
and when old Mary started preparing the walnut table which I knew came from the attic,
laying the snowy cloth, the familiar gold-band
china, the Markle silver and the candles, I was
hard put to stand it. Never was Lucy so feverish
and talkative, but to me it was a ghastly farce
with the wreck that was Will silent in his wheel
chair at the head of the table, with the nurse
cutting his meat and putting it in his mouth,
and Mary panting and wheezing from the
stairs.

Until it was over I felt I had been through hell, and when I left, it was to go straight to the Legion for a drink. So that, I knew now, was why Lucy had never written us but had rushed him to Europe before anyone in Pine Mills would find out. And all the time we thought they were living such an idyll in Italy and southern France!

As I stood at the bar I had the strange feeling that someone was staring at me from behind. I turned, but all I could see through the open door was Tom Grail looking down at me from his painting on the wall. The electric light fell on him softly. After Lucy and Will, how incredibly young and fresh and peaceful he seemed! Lucy, I remembered, had thought he always got the bad end of things and Will the good. Was it possible that Lucy was wrong? Is that what Will's eyes had been trying to tell me, that there were some who had escaped all this?

For a time I couldn't take my eyes from Tom's face. He had been born before Lucy, I reflected, and yet he was still the boy who had dove off the arch and had stood by the rail at San Francisco throwing down buttons to the girls on the pier while the Pacific sun shone warmly on his blond head. He would never be any different now.

Never could he lose the mantle of youth. When Lucy was a wrinkled old woman dying in her bed and Will remembered as the broken old soldier I had seen today, Tom and his kind would still be always young and fair.